THE CHANCE OF A LIFETIME

This Large Print Book carries the
Seal of Approval of N.A.V.H.

THE CHANCE OF A LIFETIME

SHERI COBB SOUTH

THORNDIKE PRESS
A part of Gale, Cengage Learning

GALE
CENGAGE Learning

Detroit • New York • San Francisco • New Haven, Conn • Waterville, Maine • London

GALE
CENGAGE Learning™

LIBRARY OF CONGRESS CATALOGING-IN-PUBLICATION DATA

South, Sheri Cobb.
   The chance of a lifetime / by Sheri Cobb South.
      p. cm. — (Thorndike Press large print Christian fiction)
   ISBN-13: 978-1-4104-0807-5 (hardcover : alk. paper)
   ISBN-10: 1-4104-0807-8 (hardcover : alk. paper)
   1. Women college graduates — Fiction. 2. Ex–football players
— Fiction. 3. Alabama — Fiction. 4. Large type books. I. Title.
   PS3569.O755C47 2008
   813'.54—dc22   2008011311

Published in 2008 by arrangement with Sheri Cobb South.

Printed in the United States of America
1 2 3 4 5 6 7 12 11 10 09 08

THE CHANCE OF A LIFETIME

CHAPTER 1

Her manner brisk and confident, Tara Bentley descended the staircase to the lobby of the *Harper's Corners Herald,* bid a courteous farewell to the receptionist at the front desk, and pushed open the tinted glass door leading to the street. As she made her way down the sidewalk, squinting her eyes against the autumn sun, the old-fashioned plate glass windows fronting the building reflected the wavy image of an ambitious young professional, a tall angular woman in tailored black trousers and a green velveteen blazer. Her bobbed auburn hair was as straight as her figure and swung with every step she took, softening the appearance of a rather pointed but determined chin.

As soon as she passed the large glass panes, however, her self-possession suddenly deserted her, and she broke into a run. Heedless of the curious glances of passers-by, she flung herself into the seven-year-old Civic parked on the corner and closed the door behind her. She dug in her purse for her cell phone, then flipped it open and punched a couple of buttons. A short pause, then one ring, two . . .

"Hello, Bentley residence."

"Mom, I got the job!" Tara shrieked.

"That's wonderful, honey, but you don't have to shout."

The matter-of-fact voice on the other end of the line left Tara feeling oddly deflated. "Aren't you even surprised?"

"Why should I be? I've always known you had talent. Besides," her mother added, "I saw Emma Wainwright at the grocery store yesterday — her husband Don owns the *Herald,* you know — and I told her you'd be coming in for an interview."

Tara almost dropped the phone. "Mom, you didn't!"

"Was it supposed to be a secret?" Tara could almost picture her mother's puzzled frown.

"Not a *secret,* exactly."

"We've known the Wainwrights forever, you know, and Emma used to teach your Sunday School class when you were nine years old. It's only natural that they should take an interest in your future."

Tara returned a noncommittal answer, her

sense of disappointment acute. Just once in her life, she would like to strike out on her own, to achieve something based on what she could do, not whom her parents knew. But that was the trouble. Everybody in Harper's Corners, Alabama knew everybody else. Even college had offered no change of scenery, since she had attended the nearest university branch campus in Midland, a scant twenty miles from the makeshift apartment she'd fashioned over her parents' garage.

"So, tell me about this job of yours," her mother said bracingly. "What department will you be in?"

I'm surprised you haven't arranged that, too. The thought sprang unbidden to Tara's mind, and she felt instantly ashamed of it. After all, her mother had only meant to help her, and it wasn't really her fault that she didn't understand Tara's hunger for independence. Like Tara, Dianne Bentley had grown up in Harper's Corners. But she had been content to marry and raise a family here.

Not so for Tara. For as long as she could remember, she had wanted to get away, and as graduation neared, she had eagerly put in applications at all the major dailies in Birmingham, Montgomery, Nashville, and

Atlanta. Unfortunately, every other college graduate with a degree in journalism had the same idea. After a summer spent pursuing job interviews which invariably ended in a polite but firm "don't call us, we'll call you," she had accepted the inevitable and applied for a position at the *Harper's Corners Herald,* consoling herself with the reflection that this job was only temporary, a stepping stone to bigger and better things.

And she didn't doubt for one moment that she was capable of those better things. She'd had a few short pieces published in magazines, and while they hadn't paid much, they still looked good on a résumé. Good enough, at least, to land her the job.

Or so she had thought, until now.

After promising to give her mother all the details when she returned home, she snapped the cell phone closed and turned back to look at the *Herald* building. Was it merely her imagination, or had the two-story structure actually shrunk since she discovered that her position there had more to do with family connections than writing talent? The large glass panes stared unblinkingly back at her, offering no answers.

"Some day," she muttered aloud to the silent building, "I'm going to shake the dust from this pathetic little town from my feet.

And when I do, I'm never coming back."

Before Tara reported to work on Monday morning, there was Sunday to be endured. No sooner had she settled comfortably in her family's regular pew (fifth row, piano side) than two of her mother's friends turned to speak to her.

"I hear you have a job at the *Herald,* Tara," one said.

"Don Wainwright is a good man," added the other. "I'm sure you'll enjoy working for him."

It rankled that her mother's friends already knew about her job — and knew how she got it, too, Tara didn't doubt.

"Actually, Mrs. Burney, I'll answer to one of the departmental editors," she said. "I'll get my assignment tomorrow."

"Whatever it is, I'm sure you'll do a fine job," the plumper of the two women predicted confidently. "By the way, did I tell you that Philip is going to be working in San Francisco? He'll be coming home for a couple of weeks before moving there. He's always asking about you," she added with a coy smile.

Before he had gone away to college, Philip Burney had gone to church here, too. He had been Tara's on-again, off-again boy-

11

friend since they were sixteen, but the only real pang she had felt when he had gone away was envy. Now she felt it again.

"San Francisco!" she breathed reverently, images of the Golden Gate Bridge dancing in her head. "He's lucky. I wish I could go there."

Mrs. Collins gave her a sly wink. "Maybe you will someday."

"Maybe."

That'll be the day, Tara added silently. She knew the women's intentions were good, but their well-meaning comments only added to her dissatisfaction. She half-heartedly sang along with the hymns she had known all her life, then offered up her usual prayer.

Is this all there is? she asked God. *Is this all there is for me, to be trapped here while other people go to all the places and do all the things that I've only dreamed of? Lord, I'll even become a missionary if you'll send me somewhere far away from Harper's Corners!*

But as always, there was no indication that God wished to take her up on this generous offer, and once again she went home feeling frustrated and unfulfilled.

By the time she passed through the double doors of the *Herald* building on Monday

12

morning, Tara's earlier disappointment had given way to a determination to prove herself. Her first stop was the personnel department, where she filled out the requisite forms, her hands trembling from mingled excitement and nervousness. Soon she would be following leads and gathering facts, uncovering stories of far-reaching consequence or reporting incidents of heart-tugging emotion. And in the process, she would gain experience that would help her get a job at one of the larger newspapers in Birmingham or Atlanta.

By the time the last of the forms had been completed, her nervous trembles had subsided and she was able to climb the stairs with no more debilitating symptoms than a slight case of butterflies in the stomach. As she reached the second floor, a door opened on her left, and a large bear-like man emerged. He was in his late fifties, and his genial features wore a harried expression. In one hand he nursed a cup of steaming coffee.

"Ah, Tara! Glad you made it," he said, his expression lightening somewhat as he came forward to greet her with a firm handshake. "If you've finished running the gauntlet downstairs with personnel, I'll take you to meet your new editor."

"Thank you, Mr. Wainwright."

"Call me Don," the newspaperman insisted, ushering Tara down the hall. "Here at the *Herald,* we're all one big happy family."

In proof of this assertion, he paused frequently along the way, introducing her to various reporters, photographers, and departmental editors. With each introduction, Tara wondered if this was to be her new boss. But each time, Don again took her arm and led her further along the hall.

"Frankly, Tara, your application was an answer to prayer," he confided. "One of our most experienced sports reporters is recovering from back surgery. He'll be all right, but he won't be back at work for at least three months."

"That's a shame. I hope you have a competent replacement."

"I'm sure you'll do just fine," he assured her.

As understanding dawned, Tara's dreams of journalistic glory turned to stone and settled somewhere in the pit of her stomach among the butterflies. Was *this* the opportunity she'd prayed for? What in the world was God thinking?

"Me? A sports reporter?" she sputtered. "But Mr. Wainwright —"

"Don," he reminded her.

"Don, I don't know anything about sports!"

"You're an intelligent young woman, Tara," he said soothingly. "I'm sure you'll learn quickly."

"But I don't really think I —"

"What? Just because you happen to be female? Nonsense! The growth of women's sports over the last decade has been phenomenal."

"That's another thing," Tara continued doggedly, following her employer into a large room partitioned off into numerous cubicles. "I always thought of sports reporting as, well, sort of an all-boy's club."

"And so it was, at one time. But this is the twenty-first century, and times have changed. Why, it won't be long before every newspaper in the country has at least one reporter assigned to cover women's sports. And you can bet that most of those reporters are going to be women." He broke off to regard Tara speculatively. "Oh, I get it! If it's harassment you're worried about, you can rest easy. I promise you, you'll be treated just like one of the boys."

"Just like one of the boys," Tara echoed numbly, following Don down an aisle separating two rows of cubicles.

15

"Ah, here he is! Tara, meet your new editor, Murphy Masters. Murphy, Tara Bentley, the newest member of your team."

Tara had never seen Murphy Masters before, at least not in person, but he needed no introduction. Although she had still been in grade school when Murphy had begun his assault on the Harper's Corners High School football team's record books, his reputation had preceded him. Everyone in the state knew "The Master." The former University of Alabama tight end had gone on to stardom with the Green Bay Packers until last year, when a knee injury had abruptly ended his career.

At five feet seven, Tara had always considered herself fairly tall, but the imposing figure before her made her feel uncomfortably small and helpless — an impression no doubt strengthened by the former football player's broad shoulders and well-developed biceps.

Unfortunately, any admiration she might have felt for him died the moment her eyes met his. Raking his fingers through sandy hair, he appraised his new reporter with such icy blue eyes that Tara felt as if the temperature in the room had just dropped twenty degrees. Still, she was determined not to be intimidated.

16

"How do you do?" she asked, boldly extending her right hand.

He took it, but with obvious reluctance, and when he spoke it was not to her at all, but to Don Wainwright. "She's a woman!"

"How perceptive of you," responded Tara with a kindling eye.

"That should come as no surprise," Don said. "I've been thinking of hiring a female sports reporter for some time now. I'm sure I mentioned it to you."

"I thought you were joking!" Murphy sputtered.

Don's bushy eyebrows rose, expressing mild curiosity. "Did I laugh?"

Tara's annoyance grew. She had never expected to be pampered, but they were talking about her as if she weren't even there!

"Look, Don, I don't want to cause any problems," she interrupted. "Isn't there some other department where I could —"

"Something a little more appropriate for a rookie," agreed Murphy. "Couldn't the society editor use some help covering all those garden club meetings?"

Storm clouds gathered in Tara's gray eyes. *"Garden club meetings?"* she echoed indignantly. An assignment like that would doom her to remain in Harper's Corners for the rest of her life — and beyond, as her lifeless body would no doubt be laid to rest in the cemetery behind the Harper's Corners Baptist Church.

"Tara may be inexperienced, Murphy, but she has a great deal of talent," Don said, ignoring her outburst. "I'm sure that, given time, she'll become a valuable addition to your staff."

"Unfortunately, time is the one thing I haven't got," Murphy replied, turning back to his desk and making a great show of shuffling through papers. "I've got a deadline to meet."

Don's genial expression faded, and his eyebrows drew together over the bridge of his nose. "Murphy, you've been a great asset to this paper over the last year, and because of that, I've made allowances for you that I wouldn't for anyone else. But remember, I'm still the boss."

He might have said more, but at that moment a harried-looking woman rushed up to them, the low heels of her sensible pumps clicking on the tile floor. "Oh, Don, do you have a minute? The mayor is on the line, and insists on speaking to you at once."

"I'm on my way, Joanne. If you'll excuse me, Murphy, Tara, I'll leave you two to get acquainted." Casting a speaking look at his sports editor, Don turned and followed the secretary out of the newsroom.

Tara watched him go, barely suppressing a sigh of envy. She had dreamed of fielding phone calls from people in positions of power and influence; instead, she would be relaying endless statistics about meaningless ball games.

"All right, Bentley," Murphy began, folding his muscular arms and turning that frosty blue gaze upon her, "suppose you tell me what qualifies you for sports writing."

"I graduated fourth in my class at UNA-Midland with a degree in journalism," Tara replied without hesitation. "I edited the campus newspaper, and I've had a few pieces published in magazines."

"What sort of pieces?"

Tara's confidence wavered, but she kept her chin high and looked her tormentor squarely in the eye. "A short story and a couple of poems."

As she had expected, Murphy was less than impressed with her credentials. "Great!" he muttered. "I ask for a sports reporter, and I get Emily Dickenson! Do you ever attend sporting events?"

"Every now and then."

"Play pick-up games?"

"No, but —"

"Watch Monday Night Football?"

"Well, I —"

"I see! You're just trying to make a name for yourself by being the first local woman to break into a previously male sphere."

"I didn't want to be a sports reporter at all!" Tara protested. "I'd much rather be covering meetings at city hall, or interviewing interesting people, or, yes, reporting garden club meetings. And as for making a name for myself, I seem to remember another person from Harper's Corners doing that, once upon a time."

"Be warned, Bentley, I won't cut you any slack," he cautioned.

"I don't expect you to."

Tara gave him back look for look, and felt a sense of triumph when Murphy looked away first.

"This is your work station," he said curtly, indicating a cluttered cubicle equipped with an outdated computer. "If you have any questions, you can ask Julie. She's the secretary for this department."

Julie turned out to be a vivacious blonde Tara remembered from high school. At any other time, she might have welcomed a potential friend, but in her present mood, Tara found the secretary disgustingly cheerful.

"Well, Tara?" asked Julie after Murphy had gone. "Do you have any questions?"

"Only one," Tara replied. "Is he always this charming?"

Julie's smile never dimmed. "Don't let him get to you. When he came to this newspaper last year, he didn't have any more experience than you do, and he stepped straight up to the editor's desk."

"With no previous experience?" Tara echoed distastefully. "How?"

"The bottom line, of course. Do you have any idea what it does to a paper's circulation to have a celebrity's name on the masthead? We've got subscribers from all over the state."

"I didn't know that many people followed football."

"In Alabama, where it's practically a religion? Surely you jest! Besides, even people who don't know him from his football days know about his love life. He's been romantically linked with any number of models, actresses, and pop singers. Tell me, Tara, are you familiar with a daytime soap called *Another Time, Another Place*?"

Tara nodded, taken aback by the abrupt change of subject. "I've seen it a few times. Why?"

"Do you remember a character named

21

Chelsea?"

"Who could forget her? Half the girls at UNAM wore their hair just like hers."

"At this time last year, she was poised to be Mrs. Murphy Masters."

"Chelsea?" Forget the *Harper's Corners Herald,* thought Tara. This place could rival the supermarket tabloids.

"Damaris Wade, actually. The actress who plays Chelsea," Julie explained.

"But they broke up?"

"She broke it off right after Murphy's injury. I don't know all the details, but if he's a bit less than keen on women right now, who can blame him?"

"Thanks for the warning. I'd hate to put my foot in it," Tara said, although it seemed unlikely to make much difference. Murphy Masters had already made up his mind to dislike her no matter what she said or did. As for Julie's theory that Murphy's resentment of her sprang from his experience with Damaris Wade, the very idea was ludicrous. No one with eyes in his head could possibly find any basis for comparison between herself and the gorgeous blond daytime diva.

By the time Murphy returned ten minutes later, she was busily typing, her fingers rapping out a staccato rhythm on the keyboard.

He paused behind her to study the computer screen, which displayed the immortal sentence about the quick brown fox and the lazy dog.

"What are you doing, Bentley?" he demanded, bending over her shoulder to scowl at the blinking cursor.

"Just getting familiar with the word processing program. And my name is Tara," she reminded him. "One big happy family and all that, you know."

He fixed her with an unblinking look. "You're not being paid to waste time. The Harper's Corners High School girls' volleyball team plays tonight at six. Be there, and have your story on my desk by noon tomorrow." He made as if to leave, then paused. "And one more thing: don't get too comfortable at that desk. As soon as Joe Mullins returns from medical leave, you'll be headed to another department."

Without waiting for a reply, he turned and stalked off, leaving Tara to glare at his retreating back.

"I'll be counting the days."

CHAPTER 2

At home in the modest house he'd purchased with the last of his meager savings, Murphy thumbed through the day's mail. Besides the usual bills, there was a letter from a local car dealership containing a check for the television commercial he'd recently filmed hawking pick-up trucks. Another envelope contained an effusive letter inviting him to be Grand Marshal of the Arkadelphia Christmas Parade. These occasional reminders were all that remained of the fame that had once been his.

What, he wondered, had he done to deserve this? A scant twelve months ago, he'd had a life any man would envy: an exciting, not to mention lucrative, career, an income approaching seven figures, and a gorgeous fiancée. And he'd lost it all in one fraction of a second, one freak tackle that had put a period to his pro career — his engagement too, for that matter. Dear Damaris, it seemed, couldn't disappoint her fans by marrying a has-been. She had visited him in the hospital the very next day, expressing a martyr-like determination to set him free. She loved him too much, she explained tearfully, to ask him to play second fiddle to her. All she asked was that she be allowed to keep his ring as a memento. At the memory, his lips twisted in a wry grimace. Leave it to Damaris to find a way to unload an unwanted fiancé without letting go of the three-carat rock he'd given her!

Hard upon the heels of his broken engagement had come the discovery that his agent was robbing him blind. After six years in the NFL, he should have been set for life. Instead, he'd found himself, at age twenty-eight, dusting off his journalism degree and pounding the pavement just like any other college graduate with no money and no experience. When Don Wainwright had offered him a position as sports editor, he'd thought perhaps things were finally beginning to turn around. The last thing he needed was some pointy-nosed female upsetting his painstakingly patched-up life.

Well, he couldn't stop Don from hiring her, but that didn't mean he had to make things easy for her. No, Miss Tara Bentley would get no help from him. He would treat her just as he would one of the boys, and if she couldn't take the heat, she could just get out of the kitchen.

The analogy reminded him that he was hungry. He tossed the mail aside and headed for the kitchen, where he took a frozen dinner out of the freezer and put it in the microwave. He punched a few buttons, then located a canned soft drink in the refrigerator and popped the top. The beep-beep of the microwave some minutes later informed him that his dinner was ready, and he peeled the clear plastic cover off a steaming mound of spaghetti topped with meatballs. He had just dragged up a bar stool and was about to sit down when the telephone rang. Heaving a sigh, he picked up the receiver.

"Hello?"

"Hello," came the reply. The voice was distinctly feminine. Murphy's hackles rose. "Is this Murphy Masters, the sports editor for the *Harper's Corners Herald*?"

"Yes, it is."

"Oh, good! My name is Angela Michaelson. I've been trying to reach you for days. It's about my son, Jason. He just won the Junior Bowling Championship. I thought you — the newspaper, I mean — might want to know."

Murphy grimaced. He had been dodging this particular woman's calls for two weeks, ignoring the frequent messages she left on his office answering machine in the hopes that she would eventually get tired and give up. Instead, the proud mother had tracked him down at home. It looked as if he would have to assign a reporter to the story just to get rid of her. But who would he insult by assigning such a piece of fluff? Bob Walters might do it. After all, Bob had a background in advertising; he was used to making something from nothing.

As a better solution presented itself, the corners of Murphy's mouth curled up in a demonic grin. So Tara Bentley wanted to make a name for herself as a sports reporter, did she? Well, she would have her chance.

"Mrs. Michaelson, I'm so glad you called," he said, with so much warmth in his voice that his co-workers would hardly have recognized it. "If you'll phone me at the paper tomorrow morning, I'll put you in touch with the very person you need. A new reporter, a real go-getter, and just the person to see that your Joshua —"

"Jason," put in Mrs. Michaelson.

"Jason, then, gets the recognition he deserves."

■ ■ ■ ■

While Murphy plotted, Tara sat on the bleachers in the Harper's Corners High School gym, watching a group of pony-tailed teenagers bat a volleyball back and forth over the net. It galled her that Murphy had told her to turn in her story the following day; she knew it would be more typical for a reporter to fax or e-mail the story in that night so it would make the next morning's edition. A little voice at the back of her mind pointed out that it wasn't unreasonable for an editor to want to see a new reporter's work before running it. Still, Tara suspected that nothing would please Murphy more than to find fault with her story, and she was determined not to give him the satisfaction.

Unfortunately, Tara had not been exaggerating when she told Don she knew nothing about sports. She took painstaking notes, but scribbled an equal number of question marks in the margins, indicating points to double-check before writing her finished piece.

"Well, you learn something new every day," remarked a familiar voice from somewhere over Tara's left shoulder. "I didn't know you were a volleyball fan."

"Hi, Philip." Tara moved her purse to make a place for him to sit. "What are you doing here?"

"I came to see Karen," he answered, pointing to the tall, pony-tailed blonde serving the ball over the net. "I won't get many more chances to watch my sister play."

"Hey, I heard about your new job." Tara tried to sound enthusiastic. "Congratulations! When will you be moving to San Francisco?"

Philip applauded along with the sparse crowd as the other team tried and failed to return the serve. "Not for two weeks yet. But I hear I'm not the only one with a new job. Mom says you're working for the *Herald* now."

Tara made a face. "I am. The bad news is that I'm a sports reporter. That's why I'm here."

If she had looked for sympathy, Tara had gone to the wrong place. Philip regarded her with admiration bordering on awe. "You're working for Murphy Masters?"

"You know him?"

"Know him?" echoed Philip. "When I was in junior high, The Master was my hero!"

"I hate to shatter your boyhood dreams, but your hero has feet of clay," Tara informed him bluntly.

"In what way?"

"For starters, he's got a rotten personality and a bad attitude. And do you know what's even worse?"

Philip opened his mouth to hazard a guess, but Tara didn't let him get a word in.

"I have more education and more experience than he does! While I was editing a college newspaper, what was he doing? Running around a football field bashing people's heads in!"

"Er, I hate to spoil your dramatic finish, but Murphy is — *was* — a tight end," Philip pointed out. "He didn't bash people's heads in; they bashed his."

"Well, that would explain a lot," Tara muttered darkly. "Look, since your sister plays volleyball, you must know something about it. Can you answer a couple of questions for me?"

Philip could and did, and with his help Tara was able to cross out all the question marks decorating the margins of her spiral notebook.

"Karen and the rest of the team usually go out for pizza after a win," Philip said when the match was over. "Since I'm not needed for chauffeur duty, can I walk you home?"

Tara gave a nod. "Okay."

Together they covered the two blocks to Tara's garage apartment, Philip's arm draped comfortably about her shoulders. "It's early yet," he remarked as they mounted the steps to the landing. "Mind if I come in?"

Tara shook her head. "Sorry, Philip, but not tonight. I'd like to get started on this story."

"Later, then," he said, leaning forward to give her a quick kiss. At the last second she turned, and Philip's kiss landed on her cheek instead of her lips.

He gave her a searching look. "Tara, is something wrong?"

"No, it's just that I've got a lot on my mind right now, with this new job and all. I'll see you later, okay?"

Ignoring this dismissal, Philip cut right to the point. "If you don't like the job, why don't you quit?"

"And do what?" she retorted with a derisive laugh. "Jobs don't grow on trees. At least, not around Harper's Corners, they don't."

"Then try somewhere else," Philip suggested.

"I have! I've sent résumés to Birmingham, Huntsville, Montgomery —"

31

"What about outside the state?"

She continued ticking them off on her fingers. "Atlanta, Nashville, New Orleans —"

"San Francisco?"

"No," Tara admitted, momentarily taken aback by the swift jump in geography.

"There you have it!"

"Philip, what *are* you talking about?"

"I'm talking about us. Let's get married."

"You can't be serious!"

"Of course I am! Why shouldn't I be?" Seeing Tara was not convinced, he added, "We've been dating since high school. Everybody at church has been expecting it for years."

It wasn't the wisest choice of words. No matter how tempting San Francisco might be, if there was one thing that would make Tara balk at accompanying Philip there, it was the knowledge that everyone in Harper's Corners expected her to do so. But even beyond that, there was something else, something she couldn't quite put a finger on. She and Philip had grown up together. They had been friends since they were children, and in high school they had begun dating. Philip was good-looking, fun to be around, and reliable. But then, so were golden retrievers. As much as she would miss Philip when he was gone, she couldn't shake the conviction that if she had dated him for six years and still wasn't sure if she wanted to marry him, something important was missing.

"I'm sorry, Philip," she said gently, "but I can't marry you."

Philip frowned. "Can't, or won't?"

"Either. Both. You'll always be special to me, but I can't marry you because I don't love you the way a woman should love the man she marries. You deserve better than that."

"I don't want what I deserve!" Philip growled impatiently. "I want you!"

In spite of the seriousness of the moment, Tara had to laugh. "Really, Philip, that wasn't exactly flattering."

"I'm trying to tell you that I love you!"

"No, you don't," she said, shaking her head sadly. "At least, not in the way you mean. You're moving to a strange city, and you don't want to be alone. Give it time. I have a feeling someday you'll be glad I turned you down."

"I think you're wrong, but if there's nothing I can say to change your mind —"

"Not a thing."

Philip hesitated, then held out his hand uncertainly. "Still friends?"

Tara grinned. "The best," she said, placing her hand in his.

After he had gone, though, Tara had to wonder. She'd asked God for a way out of Harper's Corners, and she'd just turned one down. Had Philip's proposal been the answer to her prayers? But surely if it was God's will that she marry Philip, she would know it. Wouldn't she?

When the alarm clock buzzed the next morning Murphy, for the first time in more than a year, did not punch the snooze button and bury his head beneath the pillow. Instead, he threw back the covers and got out of bed, yawning widely and flexing his arms over his head to banish the last vestiges of sleep before heading for the shower. By the time he reached the sports department of the *Herald,* he was whistling a jaunty tune, unaware of the trail of gawking secretaries, reporters, and other newspaper employees he left in his wake. Walking between the rows of cubicles, he discovered Tara already seated at her work station. Murphy felt a momentary pang of irritation at the sight, but shrugged it off. Nothing could dampen his good humor today, not even the discovery that Tara Bentley was at least prompt.

34

"Bentley, you'll be getting a call today from a woman named Angela Michaelson with a story," he told her. "I'll want at least twelve inches of text."

He strode over to his desk without waiting for a reply, but once there, he couldn't concentrate on his work. His patience, such as it was, was finally rewarded just before ten o'clock, when Julie answered the phone and transferred the call to Tara's line. A brief conversation followed, and although Murphy was too far away to hear anything, he watched surreptitiously as Tara tucked a strand of straight auburn hair behind one ear, then twisted the telephone cord around her little finger. The restless movements of her hands communicated her feelings as eloquently as any words could.

Not, he suspected, that she would be lacking in that department either. As she replaced the receiver in its cradle, he watched the big clock mounted on the wall at the far end of the newsroom. Four seconds had hardly ticked off before she appeared in the opening of his cubicle, her hands planted firmly on her trim hips. Behind wire-rimmed reading glasses, her stormy gray eyes flashed.

"Angela Michaelson just called," she stated without preamble. "Really, Murphy,

Junior Bowling Champion? Do I have to put my name on that?"

He shrugged. "You wanted to be a sports reporter."

"I never wanted to be a sports reporter! Don Wainwright assigned me to this department."

"Well, nobody's making you stay," Murphy pointed out.

"True," Tara retorted. "I'm out of here."

Before Murphy realized what she was about to do, she turned and marched out of the newsroom without a backward glance, pausing only long enough to snatch her purse from off her desk.

The abruptness of her departure made Murphy blink. Of course, his suggestion that she do precisely that had not been exactly subtle. He'd been hoping to make her quit from the moment he learned she'd been hired. Still, he had not expected success so soon, and he felt oddly deflated. He'd thought she would at least put up a fight; in fact, he hadn't realized until now just how much he had been looking forward to it. Nor had he realized that they'd had an audience until Julie spoke.

"Don't think you've gotten rid of her that easily, Murphy," the secretary said with a knowing grin. "She'll be back. She promised to meet the Michaelson kid at the bowling alley in half an hour."

"I knew that," growled Murphy, but he might as well have saved his breath. No one believed him, not even himself.

Jason Michaelson, Tara soon discovered, was a red-headed nine-year-old in baggy blue jeans and name-brand athletic shoes. Tara braced herself for a half-hour spent listening to the crowings of a cocky pre-adolescent, but to her surprise, he was rather bashful. Perhaps overly conscious of his mother's proud but watchful eye upon him, he answered Tara's questions in mono-syllables. At this rate, she thought, he would be old enough to qualify for the senior league before she had enough information to fill Murphy's twelve inches of text.

"Why don't we bowl a few frames?" she suggested at last in desperation. "You can show me your winning form."

As she had hoped, this suggestion found instant favor. Jason cast an eager and yet pleading glance at his mother. "Can we, Mom?"

Angela Michaelson reached for her purse. "Let me see how much cash I've got."

"I'll put it on my expense account," Tara said hastily. *If Murphy Masters wants this article, let* him *pick up the tab,* she added mentally.

She could not have found a surer way to put Jason at ease. By the time she had changed into her rented shoes and enlisted the young champion's help in choosing a ball, he had lost his shyness. When he got a strike in the second frame, he became even more willing to talk about his achievements.

"You must have a lot of experience at this," Tara remarked as they waited for the pins to be reset.

Only a few minutes earlier, this observation would have earned no more enthusiastic reply than a grunted "uh-huh," but now Jason chattered away as if he and Tara were old friends.

"I've been bowling since I was five," he said happily, and went on to relate how he had first been introduced to the sport at a neighbor's birthday party.

Tara had not had a great deal of experience in working with children, and was pleased to discover that she was quite adept at handling young boys. Now all she had to do was find a way to apply that strategy to the grown-up variety, she reflected morosely, thinking of her surly editor.

By the time they finished the tenth and final frame, Jason had beaten her soundly.

But any damage to Tara's ego was assuaged by the fact that she had a recording, carefully concealed to keep her subject from clamming up on her again, full of his eager conversation — including his unsolicited but well-meaning advice for improving her game. All of which she intended to incorporate into a story that would knock Murphy Masters's socks off.

Murphy had not sent a photographer with her, so Tara snapped a few shots with a camera borrowed from the newspaper's photography department, and then drove back to the office. Upstairs, the sports department seemed strangely empty, although a closer look revealed Julie hard at work on her computer. Shaking off the feeling, Tara sat down at her own computer and roughed out the story as she ate her sandwich. Murphy had still not returned by the time she completed the final draft, so Julie showed her how to put it in the sports "basket," a computer file where all the finished pieces were stored for editing.

By the time Murphy returned, accompanied by Don, Tara had finished all her work, and she and Julie were engaged in idle chitchat — a fact which did not go unnoticed by Murphy.

"Bentley, I need that article on the

Michaelson kid," he barked as he strode past Tara's cubicle.

"It's in your basket." Her voice was just a bit too sweet for sincerity.

"You're still fighting it, aren't you, Murphy?" Don observed as he led the way to Murphy's cubicle. "Give the girl points for promptness, at any rate."

"I'm not giving her anything until I read the piece," Murphy said, glowering behind him at Tara, who had resumed her interrupted conversation with Julie.

With Don watching over his shoulder, Murphy punched a few buttons on his keyboard, and a moment later Tara's article came up on the monitor. Murphy scanned the piece, his frowning gaze searching for flaws. Although he didn't look back, he knew that behind him Don was doing the same thing.

"What did I tell you?" Don said at last. The satisfaction in his voice was obvious.

"Okay, so she did all right with one fluff piece," Murphy admitted grudgingly. "That still doesn't mean she's got what it takes to handle a major story."

"Why not try her and see? The Braves have a home game this weekend, don't they? Send Tara to Atlanta to cover it."

"Are you kidding? That's a playoff game

with World Series ramifications!"

"How else are you going to find out what she's capable of?"

Murphy shook his head. "Not a chance, Don. I'm the one who would end up with egg on my face if she bombed."

"Oh, so this is an ego thing, is it?"

"No, it isn't!" Murphy retorted. "You didn't hire me to run a nursery school for cub reporters. I have to put the best —" He broke off in mid-sentence as an idea struck. So Don wanted Bentley to do a major story, did he? Well, he would get his wish. And when she couldn't hack it, Murphy would be rid of her. Problem solved. "All right, Don, you win. I'll have her fax her credentials for a press pass."

After Don returned to his own office, Murphy strode back down the aisle to Tara's cubicle. He paused in the opening, resting his muscular arms along the top edge of the partition.

"Bentley, do you have any plans for this weekend?"

She looked up suddenly, her gray eyes wide and startled behind her reading glasses. Too late, Murphy realized that his question sounded almost as if he were about to ask her for a date. He grimaced. He'd never had this problem with Joe Mullins.

41

"If you do, cancel them." Embarrassed at his own clumsiness, the words came out a bit more abruptly than he'd intended. "I'm sending you to Atlanta to cover the Braves. You'll need to fax your credentials in order to get a press pass. They can either overnight it to the office, or you can pick it up at the 'will call' window when you get there. Julie can give you the number."

Tara opened her mouth as if to speak, but no words came out. Murphy could only assume he'd robbed her of speech. Well, that was something, anyway, he thought with no small sense of satisfaction.

CHAPTER 3

That weekend, Tara climbed into her little white Civic, jotted the odometer reading down on her expense statement, and set out on the four-hour drive to Atlanta. She suspected — no, she was certain — that Murphy had given her this assignment in the hope that she would botch it, and the knowledge made her all the more determined to give him a story that would blow him away. Covering the Braves was unlikely to win her a Pulitzer, but it was an improvement over nine-year-old bowlers, and she intended to make the most of it.

Unfortunately, no one said it would be easy, as she discovered when, stiff and sore from four hours behind the wheel, she reached her destination and stopped at the "will call" window to pick up the media pass that would admit her to the press box behind home plate.

"Tara Bentley?" echoed the man at the

window. "I'm sorry, but we don't have a pass for a Tara Bentley."

"Maybe someone was expecting a man and got the name wrong," she suggested. "Will you look under Terry Bentley?"

He did, but returned to the window a moment. "I don't have it."

She reached for her cell phone, hoping to catch Don or, heaven forbid, even Murphy, but then remembered she didn't know their home phone numbers. "Can't I just show you some form of ID?"

He shook his head. "Sorry, but no one gets into the press box without a pass. If you want to see the game, you're going to have to buy a ticket."

With this Tara was forced to be content. She took her place at the end of the long line of humanity snaking out from the stadium, praying that the game wouldn't be sold out, even as she entertained distinctly unchristian thoughts toward her boss. An innate sense of fairness compelled her to admit that Murphy could not be held directly responsible for her lack of a press pass. Still, he was certainly the one who'd suggested she pick it up at the window. Murphy himself, as she had later learned from Julie, always had his own passes sent to the office to avoid just such a calamity.

The game was not sold out, although by the time Tara had purchased a general admission ticket, bought a program, and squeezed into her seat between an overweight man and a woman holding a squirming toddler, she had missed the opening pitch. Far more serious was the fact that when she turned on her laptop, nothing happened. Oh, she heard the familiar hum of the computer booting up, but the screen remained dark even though the green power light blinked weakly in the bright sunlight.

The bright sunlight . . .

She cupped a hand over the computer screen, and could just make out the dim shape of the manufacturer's logo. There was nothing wrong with her computer after all. The brilliant September sun simply overpowered the backlit computer screen, and there wasn't a thing she could do about it. She would simply have to take notes by hand and type the story later — inside somewhere, or even after dark.

Unfortunately, since she hadn't expected to write her story longhand, she hadn't brought any paper for the purpose. She closed the laptop and emptied the contents of her purse on top of it, but found nothing more promising than a wrinkled tissue, an empty chewing gum wrapper, and Don

Wainwright's business card. Abandoning the search, she turned her program to the page with the most white space between advertisements, and began to scribble notes. Then, in the third inning, an unexpected blow to her arm drove her hand across the paper, making a jagged black line across the words she'd written.

"Brittany! Stop that kicking!" scold the woman in the next seat, swatting the toddler's swinging leg. "Now, you tell the lady you're sorry."

Pleased to be the center of attention, little Brittany smiled sweetly and gave Tara's arm another kick.

In the bottom of the fifth, the man seated on her other side ordered a beer from a passing vendor, and in the same instant Jeff Francoeur hit a grand slam over the left-field wall. In the celebration that followed, a generous quantity of beer sloshed from the plastic cup onto Tara's lap, where it mingled with Brittany's artistic endeavors and made Tara's notes even more illegible. Tara held out her dripping program and shook it, wrinkling her nose at the strong smell of alcohol.

"You look like you're having problems."

Tara turned and saw a kindly-looking older man watching her sympathetically from his seat in the next row. "You can say that again!"

"There's an empty seat here, if you need a little more room," he offered, gesturing toward the vacant seat beside him.

He didn't have to tell her twice. Tara crawled over the back of her own seat and plopped down in the seat beside him where, to her surprise, she soon found herself spilling the whole story to a total stranger.

"And it's got to be absolutely perfect, because my editor is an ex-jock, and he hates me," she concluded dismally.

The man's eyebrows rose with interest. "Baseball player?"

"No, football. The Green Bay Packers."

"What's his name?"

"Murphy Masters."

The man nodded sagely. "Ah, now there was a player! Ambitious kid, great work ethic — at least, at first. Then his last few years, something changed. I've always said that's what happens when you give a twenty-one-year-old boy more money than he's got sense. The parties, the women — it happens to some of them. Far too many, I'd say."

"Whatever it was, *something* happened to Murphy Masters," Tara agreed. "He's got a bad attitude, that's for sure. And when he finds out I've botched this job, he'll have my head on a platter."

"Maybe this will help." Reaching into the pocket of his jacket, he withdrew a small spiral notebook.

"Oh, thank you! You're an answer to prayer," she declared, accepting it gratefully.

Behind his bifocal glasses, his pale blue eyes twinkled. "Think nothing of it. I'm an old newspaperman myself."

"Really? For what paper?"

"The *Atlanta Messenger.*"

Tara breathed an envious sigh. "I'd give anything to work for a newspaper like that."

"It'll happen," he predicted confidently. "You just do your best in the job you've got, and it'll happen."

He kept up a steady flow of small talk at intervals throughout the game, at times offering bits of advice, at other times relating anecdotes of Murphy early in his career — a Murphy who seemed to bear little resemblance to the man Tara knew. Then in the top of the ninth inning, he rose stiffly to his feet.

"Well, it looks like we've got this one won," he said. "I'm going to try to get out ahead of the crowd. You tell that editor of yours he'd better appreciate you, or some bigger paper might come along and snap you up."

"Wait! Your notebook —" Tara began, tearing out the pages she had written on.

He shook his head. "Keep it," he said with a wink, then joined the exodus of fans leaving the stadium.

It remained only for Tara to find a quiet place with wireless access where she could construct the article from her notes and e-mail the finished product in to the *Herald*. An internet café would be the logical solution, but she wasn't familiar enough with her environs to venture driving around in search of one. Just getting into the city on Interstate 20 had been adventure enough. She'd noticed a couple of hotels just across the street from the stadium; she would take a room for the night and dare Murphy to say one word about the expense.

Unfortunately, even this simple task proved easier said than done.

"I'm sorry, but we don't have any vacancies," the woman at the hotel desk told her. "With the Braves in town and the Falcons playing at home tomorrow afternoon, every hotel in the area is booked solid."

It seemed there was nothing else to do but write the article from the parking lot, and hope and pray that the hotel's wireless signal was not blocked to all but paying customers. But even this was beyond Tara's capability. When she climbed back into her car and turned on the laptop, nothing happened — no hum, no blinking green light. She pressed the power button again, and received the same lack of response. With a growing sense of dread, she remembered the faded-out screen that had greeted her first attempt at the baseball game. It wasn't possible that she had forgotten to turn the computer off — was it? If so, she was doomed, for the battery would be dead as the proverbial doornail, and the power cord was at home in her garage apartment, tucked into the bottom drawer of her desk for safe keeping.

She glanced at the clock on the dashboard. If she hurried, she could be home by nine o'clock — just time to type up her article and squeak it in just as the Sunday morning edition was going to press. She drove as fast as she dared on the unfamiliar freeways, but traffic was heavy, and an accident near the state line reduced the highway to one westbound lane, creating a bottleneck that stretched as far as the eye could see.

It was well after midnight by the time she returned to the garage apartment, but Tara had no time to sleep. She plugged in her computer, booted it up and, rubbing her tired eyes, struggled to reconstruct the game from damp, smudged notes that reeked of beer. As she crawled into bed shortly before dawn, she heard the carrier toss the morning paper onto the porch, but she didn't rush outside to pick it up. She didn't want to see the big blank space where her story should have been.

When she reached the offices of the *Herald* on Monday morning, she wasn't in the least surprised to see Murphy waiting for her at the cubicle, slapping a rolled-up newspaper against the palm of his hand.

"Did you see the Sunday paper, Bentley?" he asked, his voice ominously calm.

The ironic lift of Tara's eyebrow was heightened by the dark circles underneath her eyes. "I haven't had much time for reading."

"Believe me, this won't take long."

He handed her the newspaper. The front page beneath the fold was dominated by a public service announcement that took up a quarter of the page. Tara didn't have to be told that the space was originally allotted for the Braves' playoff game.

She closed her eyes and expelled a long sigh. "I know, Murphy, and I can explain —"

"*Explain?* Bentley, there's no excuse for this!"

"No excuse, maybe, but there's a perfectly logical explanation, if only you'd give me a chance to —"

"I've already given you a chance, at Don's insistence, and you proved what I suspected all along. You're just not right for this job."

"Well, I'd like to meet the person who *could* have gotten that story in, under the same circumstances!"

"What's the problem, Murphy?" asked Don Wainwright, coming forward to join them.

Murphy snatched the newspaper from Tara's slackened grasp and thrust it at Don. "The *problem* is that Bentley here didn't get her story in, and one-fourth of the Sunday sports page is a blank!"

The senior editor studied the blank page for a long moment, then asked, "What happened, Tara?"

"I'm glad *someone* is willing to listen to my side," Tara said, glaring at Murphy. "There was a misunderstanding of some kind, and they didn't have my press pass at the window. I had to buy a ticket to get in — you'll see it listed on my expense report — so I couldn't use my laptop. As for the people I ended up sitting beside, trust me, you don't want to know. In fact, if it hadn't been for the wonderful man behind me, I don't know what I would have done! He gave me a spiral notebook and helped me keep up with the game while I took notes by hand. I wrote the story before dawn this morning, after I got home. I knew it was too late by that time but, well, it was the best I could do."

"A heroic effort, under the circumstances," Don remarked.

"But late, all the same," put in Murphy.

"I tried my best —"

"Sorry, but trying isn't good enough," Murphy interrupted.

Don rubbed his chin thoughtfully. "I think," he said slowly, "it's time I made a change."

Murphy gave a satisfied nod.

Tara, torn between fury and despair, could only stammer, "But — but Don, you said —"

He silenced her with the lift of a finger. "Tara, your heart is undoubtedly in the right place, but you still have a lot to learn, and your editor is the logical choice to teach you."

This was clearly not what Murphy had expected. "Hold on a minute!"

"As you so succinctly pointed out, Murphy, this is a newspaper, not a nursery school," Don went on. "I'm tired of the two of you bickering like children. Until further notice, you will cover every event together, you'll write every story together, and you'll share a byline. Are there any questions?"

Stunned silence was the only response.

"Good," said Don, and returned to his office without another word, leaving the quarreling co-workers staring after him in dismay.

Murphy was the first to recover. "Now, wait just a minute!" he demanded, his long strides quickly closing the distance between himself and his employer. "You can't do that!"

Don turned to look at him, his face registering mild curiosity. "I can't? Who do you suppose is going to stop me?"

"Look, Don, you hired me to do a job here. How am I supposed to get anything done with that girl chained to my ankle?"

"Hmm, now there's a thought," remarked Don with relish. Seeing his sports editor was not amused, he added, "Murphy, there was a foul-up with her press pass. It happens from time to time. There wasn't a thing she could have done about it."

Murphy raked his fingers through his hair in a gesture replete with helpless frustration. "You don't understand —"

"I understand," Don assured him, opening his office door and motioning Murphy inside. "In fact, I suspect I understand a lot better than you do. Sit down."

Murphy sank down onto the worn vinyl sofa, while Don perched on one corner of the desk opposite.

"I believe I know why you don't like Tara Bentley, and it has nothing to do with her talent or lack thereof," the senior editor continued. "I think she reminds you of someone you used to know."

Murphy was off the sofa like a shot. "If you're going to get started on Damaris Wade —"

"Will you *please* sit down? I wasn't thinking of Damaris Wade. In fact, I can't imagine why you would assume I was."

Reluctantly, Murphy returned to his seat. "All right, who *are* you thinking of?"

"A high school kid whose football games I used to cover back in the day. Big guy, quick, with good hands. His name was Murphy Masters."

Murphy fairly bristled with outrage. "I have never borne the slightest resemblance to that scrawny female!"

"Not physically, no. But the ambition, the drive — you had that once, Murphy."

55

A brief flicker of regret softened Murphy's features. "Maybe if I hadn't hurt my knee —"

Don shook his head. "Your knee has nothing to do with it. Oh, you were going through the motions, and you probably fooled a lot of people who hadn't been watching you since junior high, but your spark was already long gone." He paused for a long moment, frowning down at his sports editor. "And I think that, more than anything else, is why I hired Tara Bentley. I thought maybe, just maybe, if you saw somebody else with that spark, you might be able to get it back."

"I'll never play football again," Murphy told him bluntly. "The surgeon who set my knee was very sure of that."

"I'm not talking about football, Murphy. I'm talking about life."

Murphy rose from the sofa once more, a brittle smile fixed on his lips. "It's a good thing you're a newspaperman, Don, because you make a lousy psychologist," he said. "Now, since you've saddled me with that Bentley girl, I guess I'd better get back there and see what I can do with her."

Don made no attempt to stop him, but watched in silence as Murphy exited the office and closed the door behind him. Alone in his office, he idly stirred the coffee in his cup and studied the closed door as if seeking an answer there.

"I wonder, Murphy, why you were so quick to make a connection between Tara Bentley and the woman you were going to marry?" he speculated aloud.

The door, its frosted glass window uncommunicatively blank, offered no reply.

CHAPTER 4

Leaving Don Wainwright's office, Murphy slammed the door with a satisfying crash, then strode past Tara's cubicle.

"Are you coming, or not?" he demanded without looking in her direction.

Tara hurried to fall into step behind him. "Am I allowed to ask where we're going?"

"To Harper's Corners High School," he answered grudgingly. "We've got to interview the football coach about Friday night's game. I'll give you a lift."

Tara's pointed chin rose in the manner Murphy was beginning to recognize all too well. "I can take my own car."

"That thing?" scoffed Murphy, recalling the battered white Honda in the parking lot.

Tara shrugged. "It gets me where I want to go."

But did it really? So far, it hadn't even gotten her out of Harper's Corners. And as she drew closer to the little car, she realized it wasn't taking her anywhere today: the left rear tire was flat.

"Oh, no!" she groaned.

Murphy knelt to inspect the damage. "Looks like you've picked up a nail. You can call a service station when we get back, but for now you'll have to ride with me. I told Coach Russell we'd be there by ten."

Knowing it would be useless to argue, Tara followed Murphy across the paved lot to his reserved parking space. A candy-apple red sports car waited there, its chrome blindingly bright in the morning sun. Murphy unlocked the doors, and Tara sank down into the soft leather seat.

"Nice car," she said in spite of herself.

"Thanks," was the curt reply.

In fact, Murphy was slightly embarrassed by the showy vehicle that had once been his pride and joy. It had been his first major purchase after renewing his contract with the Packers, and had cost more than most men his age made in a year — or even two. He had enjoyed the envious looks he'd received as he tooled around with the top down and Damaris in the passenger seat, her long silver-blond hair streaming behind her. Now the car was a taunting reminder of just how gullible he had been, thinking his charmed life would last forever.

"You talked to him?" Tara asked hopefully as Murphy expertly wheeled the car out into the street.

"Don," she reminded him, dragging him back from a world which suddenly seemed very far away. "You talked to him about making us cover assignments together. What did he say?"

Murphy shook his head. "I could hardly get a word in. His mind is made up."

They heaved identical sighs of disappointment, then Tara said, "I'll let you in on a little secret, if it makes you feel any better. You couldn't have gotten rid of me, no matter what you said. I've known Don practically all my life. He hired me as a favor to my parents," she added, a hint of bitterness creeping into her voice.

Murphy turned to regard her with mild surprise. "That's not what he told me."

"Really? What did he tell you?"

She reminds you of someone you used to know . . .

There was no way he was going to tell that to this girl with the stubborn chin and eyes the color of Lake Michigan on a rainy day.

"Don's got some idea about the paper needing a female sports reporter," he said with a shrug.

60

"So I get to be the token female. That's not much of an improvement."

"Don't take it so personally. Don hired me because he thought my name on the masthead would be good for circulation. And he was right."

"At least you're making some kind of contribution," Tara retorted. "I can't help thinking that my most important job qualification, besides being female, is the fact that Don's wife Emma taught my Sunday School class when I was nine years old."

"Sunday School," ecoed Murphy with a soft laugh that was somehow both reminiscent and faintly mocking. "I haven't been to church in years."

Tara gave a snort of derision. "I wouldn't dare miss two Sundays in a row for fear everyone I know would call to see if I was sick."

"At least you know they care about you," said Murphy, thinking of the many people whose friendship had been as short-lived as his football career.

Hearing the unexpectedly wistful note in his voice, Tara glanced curiously at him, then looked quickly away and fixed her gaze on the passing scenery. She almost wished Murphy would say something hateful. Open hostility would have been easier to handle than this unexpected glimpse of vulnerability.

They reached the high school just as the bell signaled the end of second period. Scant seconds later, the sidewalks teemed with students on their way to their third period classes. The teenaged boys eyed Murphy's sports car with undisguised envy, while the girls found the driver more interesting than the vehicle. Oddly relieved to be back on familiar footing, Tara gave a little huff of annoyance and marched ahead of him.

The coach was waiting for them in the field house.

"Murphy! Seems like old times, seeing you here," he said, offering his former player a handshake and a hearty slap on the back.

Murphy gave an exaggerated groan. "I hope that doesn't mean you're going to make me run laps again! Coach, I'd like you to meet my assistant, Tara Bentley."

"Not Jim's daughter! I'd recognize the likeness anywhere. I graduated from high school with your father, young lady. Come on in, both of you."

He led the way into a cluttered office whose main feature was a scarred desk, its surface all but hidden beneath untidy stacks of paper, a stopwatch, a nickel-plated whistle on a green cord, and an empty soft drink can. The wall behind it was papered with a large poster showing the football team's schedule for the season. Tara sat down on a metal folding chair and drummed her pencil against her knee while Murphy and his former coach exchanged reminiscences about Murphy's high school football days. Once this topic had been exhausted, Murphy asked the coach about his team's prospects for the season.

"I wish I knew," said the older man, frowning thoughtfully at his desk as if the answer were hidden somewhere beneath the clutter. "Several of last year's starters have graduated, and now our most promising running back is on academic suspension."

Murphy's eyebrows rose in alarm. "Not the Blakely kid!"

The coach nodded. "Justin Blakely. It's this new no-pass, no-play rule the school board has adopted. You flunk one course, and *fffft!* You're out."

"Is Justin Blakely here today?" Murphy asked. "Do you think he would agree to an interview?"

"We'll soon find out." Coach Russell picked up the telephone and buzzed the administrative office. "Patsy? This is Dennis

Russell. Send Justin Blakely down here, will you?"

The football coach replaced the receiver, then stepped outside to await his star player. Tara seized the opportunity to turn on Murphy.

"You brought us all this way to interview a kid who's not even going to play?"

"The no-pass, no-play rule is tough," Murphy told her. "Some people think it's *too* tough."

"And you happen to be one of them."

"I do, but that's not the point. Why not show how it affects one real-life kid?"

"You're forgetting one thing," Tara reminded him. "Don said we had to write this article together, and I happen to think the school board has the right idea. Why should Justin Blakely — or anyone else for that matter — get special treatment just because he can run or catch a ball?"

"Maybe because that might be the only chance they have at building a future," suggested Murphy.

"If you ask me, it's a pretty shaky foundation to build on, at least in terms of longevity." Too late, she remembered the abrupt end of Murphy's career. "I'm sorry. I didn't mean —"

"Believe me, you're not telling me anything I don't already know," Murphy said, his lips curling in a humorless smile.

Before Tara could answer, a tall, broad-shouldered teenager entered the office, hovering uncertainly in the doorway.

"The Master? You wanted to see me, sir?"

His demeanor was so much that of an adolescent anxious to be cool in the presence of his idol that Tara would have been amused, had the idol been anyone besides Murphy Masters.

"So you're Justin Blakely. I've heard a lot of good things about you. Come on in and sit down. I'm Murphy Masters and this is my assistant, Tara Bentley."

Shaking the boy's hand, Tara bit her tongue while Murphy alternately flattered the boy on his past achievements and commiserated with him on his current plight.

"It's a tough rule," he told Justin sympathetically. "Some people feel it ought to be done away with."

Justin's face lit up with anticipation. "And you can get the school board to do that?"

"I can't make any promises," Murphy warned him. "Besides, my assistant made a valid point just before you came in. If you want to succeed at the next level, you can't just sit around hoping somebody will cut you some slack. You've got to prove you can perform — on the field and off."

Tara's eyes opened wide, but she held her tongue.

"But, man, chemistry's *hard!*" Justin complained.

"Have you thought about getting a tutor?" Murphy suggested.

"Beg some geek to help me? No way!"

"I had a tutor at Alabama one semester." Murphy's eyes took on a reminiscent gleam. "Her name was Heather."

"Heather, huh?" Justin considered the possibility, then shook his head. "The brainy girls at my school all bark and chase cars. We're talking real dogs!"

"Don't be quick to rule them out," Murphy cautioned. "Sometimes still waters run deep."

"Well, there's this one girl in my chemistry class who's kind of cute, but she only hangs around with the other brainiacs. I wouldn't know what to say to her."

Murphy cocked a knowing eyebrow. "You're not chicken, are you?"

Before Justin could rise to the bait, Tara spoke up. "I hate to interrupt this fascinating discussion, but we did come here to do an interview. So any time you two are ready . . ."

In spite of her annoyance, Tara could not

deny a certain grudging admiration for the way Murphy handled the boy, encouraging him to get the help he needed without lecturing or talking down to him. But she didn't *like* liking Murphy, and so when they climbed back into his car and left the campus, she lost no time in reopening hostilities.

"I thought you said you didn't agree with me on the no-pass, no-play rule," she accused.

"I don't."

"But in there you said —"

"I said you had a point," Murphy reminded her. "I never said I agreed with you. They're two different things."

"Oh, this is impossible!" Tara groaned, letting her head fall back against the supple leather upholstery. "How can we write an article together when we can't even agree on what angle to take?"

"He never said we had to agree."

Tara's brow furrowed in a puzzled frown. "What?"

Murphy took his eyes off the road long enough to glance in her direction, and for once the intensity in his blue eyes was not rooted in dislike. "Don said we had to write the story together, but he didn't say anything about what kind of story it had to be."

"So?"

"So we present both sides of the no-pass, no-play ruling and let the reader decide. Sort of like a debate, only on paper."

"Aren't you forgetting one thing?" Tara asked sweetly.

Now it was Murphy's turn to look puzzled. "No, I don't think so."

"Your hand is the last one to touch any sports story before it goes to press," she pointed out. "You have the power to cut my argument to ribbons — the way you did my volleyball article, by the way — and I would never know it until I read it in the morning edition!"

Still guiding the car with his left hand on the steering wheel, Murphy raised his right hand as if taking a solemn oath. "I won't make any changes without consulting you first," he promised. "Just keep it clean, and no profanity. This is a family-oriented publication, you know."

"Believe me, Murphy, if I was likely to use profanity, you would have driven me to it long before now!"

"And as for the volleyball article," continued Murphy, ignoring the interruption, "it was way too long."

"It was not!"

"Was so."

"You never told me there was a word limit!"

"You should have asked."

A few hours later, Tara and Murphy waited expectantly as Don scrolled through the finished article displayed on Murphy's computer screen. When he reached the end, he leaned back in his chair and looked up at his two sports reporters.

"I like it," he said decisively. "In fact, I like it so much I want to make it a weekly feature."

"A weekly feature?" Tara echoed. "You mean we'll have to find something to disagree on once a week?"

"That shouldn't be a problem for the two of you," Don said. "Unless, of course, you have trouble limiting yourselves to one disagreement per week."

"We could address national sports issues as well as local ones," suggested Murphy.

Don nodded. "Exactly! We'll give the column a catchy name."

As the two men made plans, Tara felt herself losing her already tenuous control of her career. Of course the experience should make it a little easier to find another job, and the prestige of being given a weekly column so early in her career would certainly look good on a résumé. Still, the idea of a long-term commitment made her uneasy. Turning in her resignation after being given such an opportunity could be awkward, if not down right unpleasant. Don would have to find himself another female sports reporter to share ink with Murphy. For some reason her mind shied away from the thought.

Chapter 5

Once Don Wainwright made up his mind, he didn't waste any time. By five o'clock, when Murphy returned to his empty house, plans were already underway to launch the column christened "His & Hers." Murphy hadn't been surprised when Tara had objected to the name, arguing that it sounded as if she were supposed to be speaking for all women. She could do it, too, Murphy reasoned; she certainly had the mouth for it.

Inside the house, Murphy headed for the front room in search of a telephone book — not the pencil-thin volume containing the Midland/Harper's Corners listings, but the hefty Birmingham edition. He need to find a professional portrait photographer to take publicity shots.

He flipped on the light switch and entered the room. He didn't like this particular room, and stayed out of it as much as possible. The walls were covered in framed pictures of him in all stages of his football career: round-faced and chubby-cheeked, proudly clutching his first football, all the way through high school, his college days at the University of Alabama, and finally in the green and gold uniform of the Green Bay Packers. Beneath them, a bookcase held gleaming brass trophies, plaques, and yet more photographs, the paraphernalia of a life that no longer existed.

He crossed the room without looking at the football mementos, heading instead for a smaller case containing an odd assortment of books. Locating the one he needed, he pulled it out. The remaining books fell like dominos, filling the empty space. The gold lettering on one volume caught his eye, and Murphy paused.

It was a Bible. Murphy had forgotten it was there. It had been so long since he read the Bible that he had come to associate it with road games, those Gideon Bibles placed in the top drawer of hotel rooms where the Packers stayed when traveling. Now he removed it from the shelf and turned it over in his hands. He vaguely remembered that Psalms was located in the middle. Experimentally, he stood it on its spine and allowed it to fall open in his hands. It opened to Proverbs.

"It must have been even longer than I thought," he murmured aloud to no one in particular.

Scanning down the page, his gaze fell on Proverbs chapter twenty-one, verse nine: "It is better to live in a corner of the housetop, than with a brawling woman in a wide house."

Murphy figured you weren't supposed to argue with God, but there were times, mostly late at night, when he suspected that even living with a brawling woman would beat living alone. Not surprisingly, the phrase "brawling woman" brought Tara Bentley to mind, and he allowed himself a moment to imagine her in this house. What would she think, he wondered, if he were to ask her over for dinner?

Probably that he had improper designs on her skinny little person, he decided. Well, there was a difference between being lonely and being desperate. But even as the thought formed in his brain, it was ousted by a disturbingly vivid image of Tara Bentley in his arms, silenced at last by his mouth on hers as her willowy figure molded itself to his.

Murphy shut the book with a snap and returned it to the shelf. If this was what reading the Bible did to you, it was no wonder he'd stayed away from it for so long.

The new weekly column "His & Hers" debuted in Tuesday's edition, and proved to be every bit as popular as Don had predicted. The school board was deluged with letters from readers, and had responded by calling a special session to modify, though not eliminate, the no-pass, no-play requirement. Under the new guidelines, student athletes with failing grades would undergo a probationary period during which they would receive tutoring in problem areas.

"Like they say," Murphy concluded after telling Tara of the school board's actions, "the pen is mightier than the sword."

"And the win-loss record is mightier than either one of them," she remarked dryly. "I suspect the school board's decision had a lot to do with the fact that without Justin Blakely in the game, Harper's Corners lost to Midland twenty-eight to three."

The corners of Murphy's eyes crinkled, and his mouth relaxed into something approaching a grin. "It irks you, doesn't it, that so many people agreed with me?"

It did, but that wasn't the only thing she found irksome. They had progressed from high school football to the NFL, and were now seated in the press box high above the stadium. It was bad enough that Don had sent them back to Atlanta together to cover the Falcons-Packers game for the sole reason that Murphy's pro football career had produced a sizeable pocket of Green Bay fans in Alabama. But adding insult to injury was the fact that press passes for both herself and Murphy had been waiting at the "will call" window when they arrived. The smug expression on Murphy's face when he'd picked them up had suggested that anyone remotely competent should have been able to do the same thing.

Not, she acknowledged, that she was eager to give up her seat in the press box for a general admission ticket. The Georgia Dome had been built for the 1996 Olympics, and its press box featured all the latest developments in communications technology — all the things she had once envisioned for her career. Glancing around, she thought of the journalists and broadcasters from all over the world who had once worked right here where she now sat. She wondered what they were doing now — *not* covering local high school games, of that she was certain. Returning to Harper's Corners tomorrow would be quite a letdown. It was almost as if God were toying with her, allowing her teasing glimpses of the career she had dreamed of, but preventing her from having such a life of her own.

Is this all you have for me? she started to pray, when a distraction occurred on the field below. A charging Falcon linebacker chased down the scrambling quarterback and tackled him for a five-yard loss. As the quarterback staggered to his feet, the defender raised both fists over his head and twitched his hips in a sort of jock belly-dance.

"Who's *that?*" Tara asked Murphy, forgetting for the moment that she was annoyed with him.

"Lance Lamborino."

Tara nodded. "I remember reading about him while I was doing my research for the game."

"I don't doubt it. He's one the best linebackers in the league. He was drafted the same year I was."

Tara cocked an eyebrow at him. "Is he a friend of yours?"

"Hardly. Lance is an obnoxious jerk if there ever was one. Besides his posturing on the field, he'll say or do anything to offend people, just to get a mention on ESPN."

"Well, we can't all have your charming

personality," Tara noted cynically.

"You think I'm exaggerating? All right, you can interview him in the locker room after the game."

Tara's gray eyes flew open wide. "Me? In the locker room with a bunch of half-naked men?"

Murphy's lip curled. "What's the matter, Bentley? Can't cut it?"

"All right," Tara said, her eyes glittering dangerously. "I'll do it."

As soon as the final horn sounded, Tara, true to her word, gamely joined the flock of reporters heading for the locker room where the players, fresh from the showers, would grant post-game interviews. But as she entered the cavernous network of corridors beneath the stadium, her steps began to drag. For the first time it occurred to her that in accepting Murphy's challenge she had played right into his hands. Still, her pride wouldn't allow her to back out, so she set her jaw, squared her shoulders, and marched bravely on.

As she entered the room where the other reporters were gathering, she sensed a presence behind her. Glancing over her shoulder, she saw Murphy following a few feet away. She waited to allow him time to catch up.

"You came, too?" she asked warily. "I thought you'd be covering the Packers."

"Believe me, Bentley, I wouldn't miss this for anything," he assured her.

Tara was not reassured. Her suspicions solidified into certainty a few moments later, when the players filed out of the showers. Most of them were decently if sketchily attired in sweats or warm-ups. The single exception, Lance Lamborino, swaggered into the group with drops of water still dripping from his black hair and glistening on his bare torso. The white terry cloth towel riding low around his waist provided his only covering.

"Oh, dear," Tara said faintly.

"Did I mention Lance is God's gift to women?" Murphy murmured just above her ear. "It's true; just ask him."

This flippant remark presented another problem. "If I'm supposed to be interviewing him, what do I ask him?"

Murphy shrugged. "Ask him anything you like."

As the crowd of reporters bombarded the athletes with questions, Tara bolstered her courage and waited for a brief lull. When her opening came, she grabbed it.

"Lance, your quarterback sack in the third quarter really changed the momentum of the game. Would you describe that play?"

"Describe it?" Lance gave her a long, appraising look. "Step up here, baby, and I'll give you a demonstration."

Tara sensed rather than saw Murphy stiffen behind her. Quickly, she attempted to divert Lance in a safer direction. "You now lead the league with twelve sacks on the year. To what do you credit your success?"

With slow, arrogant steps, Lance walked toward Tara until he was close enough to touch her. "I just have a natural talent for the sack," he said, reaching for the knot that held his towel in place. "Care to try me?"

Before she could respond, Tara found herself thrust rudely aside as Murphy drove his fist into Lance's boastful mouth. With the blow, the locker room erupted in chaos.

"Fight!" someone yelled.

"Call security!" bellowed someone else as Lance lunged for his attacker.

"If it isn't Murphy Masters, the has-been," he panted, spitting blood. "I thought I already put you out of this game once."

The other players entered the fray, trying to pull the two men apart, while photographers and television cameramen jostled each other for a better angle from which to catch the action. Tara could only stare in horror as a new thought occurred to her: how was she going to explain this to Don?

"Nice going, Murphy, but you forgot one thing," Tara said, holding a plastic bag filled with crushed ice against Murphy's rapidly swelling jaw. "You're supposed to *report* the news, not make it. You're lucky he didn't file assault charges."

Murphy, sitting on the edge of her hotel-room bed, submitted reluctantly to her attempts at first aid. "He wouldn't dare. He knows you could counter with sexual harassment." He frowned. "I shouldn't have sent you in there. I knew what Lance was like, even if you didn't."

"It's not like you held a gun to my head," Tara objected.

"On the bright side, at least Lance gave us something to write about next week in the column."

"Oh?" Tara asked distractedly, searching through her overnight bag for something to hold the ice pack in place. "What's that?"

"Women in the locker room. It's been the law for, what, twenty years now. But as far as I know, nobody's ever gone back and done a follow-up study on how it's worked out."

Arrested, Tara looked up from her bag.

"Surely you're not suggesting that women should be banned from doing post-game interviews because of jerks like Lance Lamborino!"

"Surely *you're* not suggesting that women ought to have to put up with that sort of thing!"

"No, but plenty of women work with obnoxious jerks every day. Believe me, I know," she added with a hint of a smile. "If we give up and get out, the jerks win. Besides, I could have handled him."

Murphy gave a snort of derision. "Yeah, right."

"I could have, if you hadn't interfered," Tara insisted.

If you're so sure of that, why did you prop open the door to your hotel room? Murphy wanted to ask. *Were you afraid you couldn't handle* me? But as Tara anchored the ice pack in place, he was distracted by a more urgent question.

"You're using *pantyhose?*"

"Sorry, but they were the only thing I could find to tie the ice pack in place. It's a woman thing. Men use duct tape for emergency repairs, women use pantyhose." She looped the stockings under his chin and tied them in a knot on top of his head, then stepped back to admire her handiwork.

"There! You probably wouldn't want to wear it out in public, but it ought to keep the swelling down."

The bed springs creaked as Murphy rose to his feet. "I'll try to get to my room without being seen."

Tara followed him as far as the door. "Are you sure you don't need an aspirin? I've got some in my purse."

"I'll be fine. I'll see you in the morning."

"Goodnight, then. And Murphy —"

"Yeah?"

She smiled uncertainly. "Thanks. For sticking up for me, I mean."

"You're welcome," he said, but the door had already clicked shut.

Murphy had hardly reached his own room when the telephone rang. The sound, unnaturally loud in the small room, startled him. Quickly he scanned the room and located the phone on a small table beside the bed.

He picked up the receiver. "Hello?"

"Murphy, Lance here."

"How did you know where to find me?" Murphy asked, taken aback.

"I overheard you telling the security guard where you could be reached. Listen, I just wanted to apologize for putting the moves on your main squeeze. I didn't know."

"Tara Bentley is my *assistant,* Lance."

"Oh, is that what they're calling them these days?" Murphy could hear the skeptical amusement in the linebacker's voice.

"I'm telling you, Lance, there is nothing going on between me and that girl!"

"Okay, okay, I believe you," Lance assured him. "I have to admit, she's not exactly your type."

Murphy had thought the same thing himself, more than once. Why, then, did it nettle him so to hear Lance say it out loud?

"Look, Murphy," Lance continued, "I don't know how to say this, but if you're sore at me for that tackle last year, I think you should know that I didn't do it on purpose."

"That's not what you said at the time," Murphy reminded him.

"Yeah, well, I do have a certain image to maintain." To Murphy's surprise, Lance actually sounded embarrassed.

"I've seen the film, Lance, more than once." In fact, they'd shown it over and over again on ESPN. "What happened to me was a freak accident, a fluke. I knew that all along, even when you were mouthing off about what you'd done."

"So tell me," Lance said, apparently satisfied that Murphy believed him, "if you don't blame me for what happened, and you're not interested in that girl for yourself, why did you light into me the way you did tonight?"

Murphy pondered the question for a long moment before replying, "I'll tell you just as soon as I figure it out myself."

CHAPTER 6

Riding the wave of success, Don began an aggressive campaign for the new weekly feature. Within two weeks of its debut, every highway within a fifty-mile radius of Harper's Corners boasted a billboard featuring a larger-than-life representation of Tara and Murphy standing back to back, arms folded across their chests, glaring at one another over their shoulders.

The investment paid off. Besides increasing sales in outlying areas, the publicity made local celebrities of Tara and Murphy. Soon the residents of Harper's Corners and its environs began to look for the duo at all local sporting events. Their constant togetherness, combined with the combative tone of their column, gave rise to rumors that their partnership went beyond the professional.

But as with so many rumors, no one bothered to ask the subjects about their relationship, and so Tara had no idea what was being said about her until several weeks later, when Julie stuck her head over the partition of Tara's cubicle.

"You have a visitor, Tara," she said with a coy smile.

Before Tara could ask for identification, Philip's grinning face appeared over the partition.

"Philip!" cried Tara, genuinely delighted to see her old friend. "What brings you here?"

"It's Mom's birthday," he said. "I thought I would surprise her."

"I'd guess you succeeded. You sure surprised me!"

"Looks to me like *you're* the one who's full of surprises," Philip said, retrieving the rolled-up newspaper he had tucked under his arm and handing it to her. Tara could tell at a glance that it was much thicker than the twelve-page *Harper's Corners Herald.*

"What's this?" she asked as she took the paper.

"Just look."

She unrolled it and saw that it had been folded open to page four of the sports section. She didn't recognize the article right away, since the headline had been changed, but soon a familiar byline leaped off the page: "by Murphy Masters and Tara Bentley for the *Harper's Corners Herald,* reprinted by permission." Scanning the columns of text, she recognized last week's "His & Hers" column about the ill-fated locker room interview.

Tara's squeal of elation could have been heard all over the building, so it was hardly surprising that it reached the ears of Murphy, who was just passing her cubicle on the way to his own. He glanced in and saw Tara with a man he didn't recognize. Since the stranger's back was to him, he couldn't see the man's face, but Tara obviously knew him well. In fact, she gazed up at him with a smile that was blinding in its radiance. Something sharp wrenched at Murphy's midsection. Suddenly recalling a piece of unfinished business, he quickened his steps. When he reached his desk, he pulled open the top drawer and removed a tangle of light brown nylon. Stuffing it into his pocket, he retraced his steps to Tara's cubicle.

"Before I forget, Bentley," he began, removing the filmy mass from his pocket, "I believe this belongs to you."

Tara tore her eyes away from the printed page long enough to recognize her own stockings dangling from Murphy's fingers. "Oh, thanks. I'd forgotten all about them."

Philip's jaw dropped open, and he gaped open-mouthed from Murphy to Tara and back again. Tara, seeing his reaction and realizing too late the conclusion to which he had jumped, stuffed the incriminating evidence out of sight.

"Look, Murphy!" she said hastily. "We made page four of the *San Francisco Chronicle*!"

Murphy bent over the newspaper Tara held, but his gaze remained firmly fixed on the visitor, who stared back at him with unabashed curiosity. "And you are — ?"

"This is Philip Burney, an old friend who recently moved to San Francisco," Tara told him. "Philip, Murphy Masters."

"Pleased to meet you." The two men shook hands, all the while eyeing one another speculatively. "Now, would it be too much trouble to continue this visit after five o'clock? We have a newspaper to get out, you know."

"Come on, Philip. I'll walk down with you," Tara added hastily, embarrassed by Murphy's rudeness.

As they descended the stairs to the ground floor, Philip turned to grin at Tara. "Yep, you're just full of surprises."

"It's not what you think!"

Philip's grin broadened. "Oh, you don't

have to explain anything to me. I understand perfectly."

He was so far off base, Tara had to laugh. "You think there's something going on between Murphy and me?"

"Well, after the warm welcome he gave me back there —"

"You thought he was jealous? Sorry to disillusion you, but he's just naturally obnoxious."

"Oh, come off it, Tara! Remember, I saw the billboards. If you two were striking any more sparks, those things would burst into flames!"

"Sparks?" echoed Tara as her laughter gave way to chagrin. "Murphy and me? Are you crazy?"

"No, and I'm not blind, either. But it looks like I may have been a bit premature, so I won't tease you," Philip promised, giving her a chaste peck on the cheek before exiting the sunlit lobby.

"He's out of his mind," Tara muttered aloud. He would have to be, to think anything but the barest civility existed between her and Murphy Masters. And yet . . .

She thought of the billboard on Highway 96, which she passed every day on her way to work. There was a certain playful quality about it which she supposed might be mistaken for flirtation by people who didn't know any better. It was probably a result of that back-to-back pose, or maybe it was a trick of the lighting. In any case, Philip had mistaken it for more — *much* more. With growing horror, Tara suspected Philip probably wasn't the only one to make that particular mistake. Certainly that would explain the knowing smiles cast her way by some of the older ladies at church — and Philip's mother's unaccustomed coolness toward her last Sunday. Tara stifled a groan. Did the whole town think she was romantically linked with Murphy Masters?

The answer appeared to be "yes," as Tara discovered that Friday night when she and Murphy climbed the bleachers toward the press box overlooking Harper's Corners High School's football stadium. Several observers followed their progress with interest, one going so far as to point a finger in their direction and shout, "There they are!"

Once inside the press box, Tara set up her laptop computer on the painted plywood countertop beneath the window. Here, at least, they were safe from curious stares, but the damage had been done. Tara was acutely aware of Murphy's physical presence in a way she had never been before. His broad torso seemed to fill the cramped room, and when he leaned down to look over her shoulder at the small computer screen, her fingers stumbled on the keys. Within the confines of the press box, it was dangerously easy — and dangerously pleasant — to imagine that the rumors were true. The night air was crisp with the promise of winter, and as a chill breeze wafted through the open windows, Tara needed only a very little imagination to picture herself and Murphy snuggled beneath a plaid stadium blanket, sharing a thermos filled with steaming hot chocolate.

If Murphy suffered from similar hallucinations, he gave no sign as he led the way back down the bleachers to ground level. As they reached the chain-link fence separating the football field from the stands, a shout made them turn.

"Murphy! Murphy Masters!"

A teenaged boy took the bleachers two at a time in his haste to reach them. As he drew nearer, Tara recognized Justin Blakely.

"Justin!" Murphy said, apparently reaching the same conclusion. "How's it going?"

"Great!" said the boy, slightly winded from his hasty descent. "This is my last week of academic probation, and by next Friday, I'll be able to play again."

"Wait up, Justin!" a feminine voice called.

A girl about Justin's age gingerly descended the bleachers. Her long dark curls bounced with every step, spilling over the collar of a letter jacket several sizes too big.

Justin grinned sheepishly. "If you've got a minute, Murphy, there's somebody I'd like you to meet." He waited a moment for the girl to reach them, then took her hand and drew her into the group. "This is Jennifer. She's been helping me out with my chemistry."

"Nice to meet you," Murphy told Jennifer, and Justin winked broadly behind her back.

"Anyway, I didn't want you to get away before I'd had a chance to thank you for everything. I just wish there was something I could do to pay you back."

"You can pay me back by keeping your grades up," Murphy said. "And good luck in next week's game."

Justin grinned like a man with a secret. "Thanks. Good luck to you, too."

"Why did he wish you luck?" Tara asked, bewildered.

"I guess he figured I needed it," Murphy said with a shrug as he watched the two teenagers walk away hand in hand. "Now, if you don't mind, we'll stop by my house first and fax this in. Then I'll take you home."

Traffic leaving the stadium was heavy as always, since Harper's Corners offered little else to do on a Friday night, but Murphy's red convertible inched its way forward until at last they reached the open road. A short time later, they drew up before a modest brick home, its windows dark and unwelcoming.

"This will only take a minute," Murphy said, shutting off the engine. "You can come in if you like."

Murphy led the way to the front door and, after fumbling for a moment with the key, turned on a light and stepped aside for Tara to enter.

Tara didn't know what she had expected Murphy's house to look like — perhaps a showy contemporary with lots of chrome and glass and black lacquer, certainly something as showy as the car he drove. But this house had the look of a furnished rental: functional yet devoid of character, betraying nothing of its owner's personality. From somewhere in the house, the ticking of a clock sounded loud in the stillness, and Tara searched for something to say to break the silence.

"How long have you lived here?" she asked.

"Almost ten months," he answered. "I

bought this place right after I moved back to Harper's Corners."

"Oh."

There seemed to be very little to say after that, and silence descended once more.

"Give me a minute to crank the computer up, and we'll be off," Murphy said, switching on the light in a room furnished as a home office. But as he flipped the power switch on the computer, the telephone on the desk rang, the shrill sound shattering the illusion of a house at rest.

"Excuse me for a minute, will you?" Murphy said over his shoulder to Tara, then picked up the receiver. "Hello?"

While Murphy took his call, Tara, left waiting in the hall, passed the time by glancing around at as much of the house as was visible by the few lights burning. The light from the office spilled through the open doorway, casting a diagonal band of light into the room opposite. The warm gleam of brass caught Tara's eye and, her curiosity aroused, she entered the dimly lit room.

Here, it seemed, was the essence of the house's owner. The room contained no couches or chairs, as if no one would wish to linger there. But the walls were lined with bookcases, and these groaned under the weight of countless plaques, trophies, and framed photographs. Most of these were of Murphy in various football uniforms, from Harper's Corners High School's blue and white to the crimson jerseys of the University of Alabama and, finally, the green and gold of the Green Bay Packers.

But it was not the football pictures that held Tara's attention. For in between them was a photograph of Murphy in full tuxedo with white tie and tails, his arm draped about the waist of a stunningly beautiful woman in a low-cut sequined gown that hugged every curve of her body. In her arms she cradled a small gold statuette of a winged woman holding aloft an open sphere: Damaris Wade of *Another Time, Another Place,* with the Emmy Award she'd just been presented for Best Actress in a Daytime Drama. If the people of Harper's Corners could see this photo, Tara thought, they would know just how absurd was the suggestion that Murphy Masters would ever look twice at her.

As she reached up to return the photo to the shelf, a broad shadow blocked the light from the room across the hall, and a moment later the overhead light sprang to life.

"What are you doing in here?" demanded Murphy.

CHAPTER 7

Tara's heart gave a startled leap, and the framed photograph slipped through her nerveless fingers and fell to the floor with a crash.

Stammering incoherently, she made a vague motion in the direction of the brass trophies, now gleaming in the light. "They were just — I wondered what —"

"If I'd wanted you in here, I would have invited you!" Murphy snapped.

"Oh, so this is holy ground, is it? Should I have taken off my shoes?" After the confusing jumble of emotions she had been prey to all evening, the familiar anger felt safe, even comforting. As long as she was furious with Murphy, she didn't have to analyze why the sight of him with another woman should be so disturbing. "Good grief, this place is a mausoleum! It's no wonder you're so bitter."

"How I choose to live my life is none of

your business!"

"When your bad attitude makes my life a misery, it becomes very much my business! For heaven's sake, Murphy, get rid of this stuff and start living again!"

"Why don't you go back to Sunday School and leave me alone?" he growled.

"All right, I will, "Tara said, her voice saccharine-sweet. "I'd invite you to come to morning services, but the roof would probably cave in." She brushed past him and retraced the hall back to the front door.

She was back again a moment later, stiff with injured dignity. "I don't have my car."

"I'll drive you," Murphy said grudgingly, and followed her out of the house.

Without a word, they climbed into Murphy's red sports car and soon were on their way.

"Slow down," said Tara as the speedometer needle crept past sixty. "I'd rather get home late than not at all."

"I'll drive as fast as I please," retorted Murphy through clenched teeth, but he eased his foot off the accelerator anyway.

Arriving at Tara's house, Murphy bade her a curt "good night" and watched with suppressed impatience the gentle sway of her hips as she climbed the stairs to the apartment over her parents' garage. The nerve of her, a kid barely out of college, trying to tell him how to run his life! He brooded over the injustice of her accusations all the way home. The very idea, that she should accuse him of making her life a misery! What did she think *she* had done to *his?* As for the church roof caving in if he were to show up, that was a lie, and he had half a mind to prove it to her.

Back inside his own house, he paused at the door of his trophy room. In his anger, he had forgotten to turn the light off, and now it sparkled off the fragments of broken glass littering the floor. He glanced at the clock on the wall. It was almost midnight. He'd clean up the mess in the morning.

Right after he took his suit to the dry cleaner's.

On Sunday morning, Tara rose from her pew to join in singing the doxology, although with something less than the desired enthusiasm. It was difficult to be thankful for blessings received when all she could see was the look on Murphy's face, all she could hear was the sound of his voice ordering her to get out of his house.

During the interminable weekend, she had managed to convince herself that Murphy was entirely to blame for the ugly little scene

98

that had taken place there. But here, in the church where she had been baptized as a child, she was forced to be more honest both with herself and with God. Murphy's behavior may have crossed the line, but she'd given him plenty of provocation.

Tara had never enjoyed admitting she was at fault, but now a bitter pill was made more bitter still by the question she could no longer avoid: why had she reacted so strongly to a photograph of Murphy with the actress he had once planned to marry? Unwilling to admit the answer, Tara welcomed the diversion offered by the church doors opening to admit a latecomer. Glancing back at the tardy worshipper, she was stunned to discover Murphy Masters hovering irresolutely on the threshold.

Pausing in the doorway, Murphy accepted the church bulletin offered by an usher, buying time while he scanned the congregation in search of a familiar face. Painfully aware of the curious stares leveled in his direction, he resisted the urge to run his finger beneath a tie that suddenly felt too tight. Still, he could not suppress a sigh a relief when he spotted Tara staring back at him with an expression in her wide gray eyes that might have meant anything from amazement to abject horror. Giving a tug to the coat of his pin-striped suit, he advanced down the aisle until he reached her pew.

"Is this seat taken?" he whispered, slipping in to stand beside her.

"It is now," she replied.

It was hardly a warm welcome, yet she did shift slightly to make more room for him.

The singing of the doxology was followed by the opening prayer, rendering further conversation impossible. But when the "amen" was said and they resumed their seats, Murphy rolled his eyes upward to glance pointedly at the ceiling.

"So far, so good," he murmured.

"Shhh!" hissed Tara, glaring at him.

Not another word passed between them, but that didn't mean Murphy wasn't thinking about her. He found himself watching her out of the corner of his eye, and thinking how different she looked. Tara always wore tailored jackets and slacks to work, but today she wore a soft blue-green thing in the wraparound style only a flat-chested woman could get away with. Somehow instead of calling attention to her shortcomings, it gave her an air of soft femininity that he'd never noticed before. Of course, no man who had ever seen Damaris Wade in a tight-fitting sequined gown could ever consider Tara Bentley beautiful. Still, there was something intriguing about her, something that beckoned him to take a closer look. He'd been aware of it for longer than he cared to admit — and never more so than last night, when he'd ordered her out of his house.

He winced at the memory. Maybe she was nosy and meddlesome, but he had the uncomfortable feeling that she might also be right. And that, more than anything else, was what had made him fly off the handle.

The choir began to sing a familiar hymn, and as he listened to the long-forgotten lyrics, Murphy was struck by how much his life had changed since he'd last been in church. It was useless to wish he'd handled things differently with Tara. There were no second chances. If the last year had taught him anything, it was that. He had every reason to be angry with God for giving him a taste of fame and fortune only to snatch it all away at the height of his success. Why, then, was there this unexpected sense of peace after months of misery? Was it the place, or the person beside him, or perhaps some combination of the two?

Whatever the cause, it was a feeling Murphy had not realized he'd missed until today, and he was reluctant to let it end.

After the closing prayer, he turned to Tara and shoved his hands into the pockets of his pants.

"Well, the roof didn't fall in," he remarked.

"No, but I nearly did when I saw you come in." Her smile was hesitant, and he knew that whatever else he might have hoped to achieve by coming here, he at least had the satisfaction of knowing he'd thrown her off balance. "Why did you come, Murphy?"

He shrugged. It was a question he didn't care to examine too closely. He would much rather speculate on whether the stockings encasing her slender, shapely calves were the same ones she'd used to anchor the ice pack to his swelling jaw. "What else is there to do around Harper's Corners on a Sunday morning?" he hedged. "Say, do you want to stop somewhere and get a bite to eat?"

She shook her head. "My grandmother is coming for dinner. It's her birthday, so Mom's pulling out all the stops." An awkward silence descended, but Murphy made no move toward the door. "You can come eat with us, if you'd like."

Murphy knew she'd only made the offer to fill the void, which had reached an uncomfortable length. A considerate person, he thought, would understand this and politely decline. Yet some streak of mischief made him nod. "I'd like that. Can I give you a lift?"

Taken at a disadvantage, Tara could only thank him for the offer and allow him to lead the way to the church parking lot, where his bright red sports car waited. As Murphy opened the passenger door for her to climb in, she noticed with a sinking heart the interested gazes of several church members turned in their direction. It was not until they reached Tara's house, however, that she remembered idle curiosity would be the least of her troubles.

"Looks like quite a gathering," Murphy remarked, parking his car on the grass beside a dark blue sedan whose driver, like Murphy, had arrived too late to find a spot on the paved driveway.

"Murphy," she began haltingly as he switched off the ignition, "about Grandma. When she sees you, she's going to think — I mean, she's always telling me I ought to —"

Murphy smiled at her, the first time she could remember him doing so. "I know what you mean," he said. "I've got a grandmother, too."

"Well, then, I guess we'd better get it over with." Tara gave him a shaky smile before leading the way up the front porch steps and into the house.

Tara's maternal grandmother was a sprightly woman whose trim figure, stylish clothes, and frosted blond hair belied her advancing years. She clung to the belief that, although her children and grandchildren remembered the day of her birth, they were not sure of the year and as a result had no idea how old she was. The family members, for their part, were well aware that she had just turned seventy-two, but loved her too much to shatter this harmless delusion, and so played along. Murphy hung back while Tara greeted the older woman with an affectionate hug and a kiss on her powdered cheek.

"I've brought a guest along, Grandma," Tara said, motioning him forward. "This is Murphy Masters. Murphy, this is my grandmother, Libby Clark. Just don't ask how old she is. It's one of the world's great unsolved mysteries."

"Happy birthday, Mrs. Clark," Murphy said, stepping forward to shake hands with the birthday celebrant.

"Oh, my!" exclaimed Libby, glancing mischievously at her granddaughter. "Where did you find this one, Tara?"

"Murphy is the sports editor at the *Her-*

ald," Tara explained, thankful that she had warned Murphy in advance. "He's my boss."

In addition to Libby, there were several aunts and uncles to be introduced before the group gathered around the dining room table. The overflow, which included Tara and Murphy, were banished to a card table set up in the corner.

"Just like I was still ten years old," Tara complained loudly, and Murphy had the impression that this, too, was a family joke. "How old do I have to be before I'm promoted to the grown-ups' table?"

"Not until someone dies to make room for you," an uncle retorted, and instantly an uncomfortable silence fell over the group. "I'm sorry, Mother, I didn't mean —"

"Nonsense!" scolded Libby. "I'm not so fragile that no one can mention the 'd' word in my presence. In case you're wondering, Murphy, my husband Frank died last winter, and my well-meaning family thinks that if they don't mention him, I won't notice he's gone. Ridiculous, I know, but their intentions are good."

"Oh, dear," sighed Dianne, Tara's mother. "Are we really that transparent, Mother? And we so wanted today to be a happy day for you!"

"It is, honey," Libby assured her. "Any time I can be with my family is a good time. I enjoyed church services, too. I know I don't go as often as I once did, but I hate sitting with all those old ladies! And I *especially* hate coming home to an empty house!"

"I can relate to that," Murphy remarked.

"Oh, no, you can't," Libby informed him. "Any man your age with an empty house has no one but himself to blame. How old are you? Twenty-four? Twenty-five?"

Although Libby disliked being asked her own age, she apparently had no qualms about asking other people the same thing. Suddenly Murphy knew where Tara had inherited her outspokenness. "Twenty-eight," he said.

"A regular Methuselah, in fact. You'd better get married soon, before you're too decrepit. Look at Tara, now," she commanded. "She inherited my bone structure. She'll age well."

"If you're any indicator, she certainly will," Murphy agreed, sending Libby into delighted whoops of laughter.

Tara wanted only for the floor to open up and swallow her. Since this seemed unlikely to occur, she settled for staring down at her plate and rearranging a pile of fluffy mashed potatoes with her fork.

She knew Murphy had earned a certain reputation as a ladies' man during his NFL days; after all, she'd occasionally flipped through *People* magazine at the hair salon. Common sense would suggest that if even half the rumors were true, he must possess more charm than he chose to show on the job. Now, witnessing the full force of his magnetism for the first time, Tara could readily believe that the reports were, if anything, underrated.

After dinner and birthday cake, the various members of the family began to scatter. The men shuffled off to the den to watch television while the women cleared off the table. Tara's mother gathered all the dirty plates onto one stack.

"I'll take that, Mrs. Bentley," Murphy said, picking up the stack and taking it to the kitchen. Tara was already there, watching the kitchen sink fill with sudsy water while she attempted to tie the strings of a checkered apron behind her back.

"You've got that thing so knotted, you'll never get it off again," Murphy observed.

He set the dirty dishes on the counter, then took the tangled apron strings. The gesture was cozily domestic, the touch of his hands disturbingly intimate. Disconcerted, Tara edged away.

"Hang on, I'm almost finished," Murphy said, pulling her back by tugging on the strings. "At least give me credit for not using duct tape. Or pantyhose."

"Speaking of which —" began Tara with a kindling eye.

"No, no," he said, grinning at her. "Not in front of your relatives."

As if on cue, one of Tara's aunts entered the kitchen. "I'll take over from here," she said cheerfully. "Do you want to watch TV, Murphy? If I know anything about men, they've found a football game on. Or have you had enough of that?"

Murphy shook his head. "Thanks, but I'd better be going."

"I'll do the dishes, Tara. You can show Murphy to the door."

Tara was quite certain that Murphy could find the door without any help from her, but having been dismissed from the kitchen, she had no choice but to give in gracefully.

"The wind is picking up," she remarked as they stepped onto the front porch. Winter will be here soon."

"And then comes basketball."

Tara wasn't quite sure if he was joking or not. "Is that all the season means to you? What sport comes next?"

Murphy shrugged, but didn't answer. "And what does it mean to you?"

"Holidays. Thanksgiving. Christmas. Spending time with family."

"With your family, I can see why. Thanks for sharing them with me."

Murphy dug his hands into the pockets of his pants and fumbled with his car keys. Tara recalled what he'd said earlier about going home to an empty house, and was surprised to discover that Murphy was reluctant to leave. For the first time, she was struck by how little she really knew about him apart from his reputation as a celebrity.

"What about your family, Murphy?" she asked. "I know you grew up in Harper's Corners, but you don't seem to have any relatives around."

"Most of them died before you were born," he said, as if he were sixty years older than she instead of six. "My mom left my dad shortly after I was born. She'd grown up in Birmingham, and decided small-town living wasn't for her. I was told she died a few years later in a nightclub fire. My dad died of cancer when I was two."

"I'm sorry," Tara said softly.

Murphy looked puzzled. "There's no reason for you to be. I don't remember either one of them, so I never really missed them."

The poignancy of that matter-of-fact statement seemed plenty reason enough for Tara, but she sensed that her pity would not be appreciated. "Who raised you, then? Surely you must have had someone."

"My grandmother — my dad's mother."

"She's still living?" Tara seemed to remember him speaking of her in the present tense.

Murphy nodded. "When she's not traveling, which isn't often, she lives in a retirement community in Florida. We're not as close as you and your grandmother seem to be, but that's okay. I figure she's raised two generations of kids; now it's her turn to do what she wants to."

"Well, any time you need relatives, you know where to come. I've got more than enough to go around."

"I might just take you up on that someday."

Murphy's smile was uncertain, not at all like the confident charmer who had won over her grandmother so easily. It made Tara feel uneasy without knowing exactly why.

"Well, I guess I'll see you tomorrow, then," she said, needing to fill the lengthening silence.

"Tomorrow," Murphy echoed, then bent

and kissed her lightly on her parted lips before crossing the lawn to his parked car.

It was negligible as kisses go, ending almost before it began. Tara might have thought she imagined it, had it not been for her rapid shallow breathing and the pounding of her heart. And yet it was real, so real that she stood alone on the porch for several long moments after Murphy drove away, holding the back of her hand to lips that still tingled.

When at last she went back inside, the hushed voices of her female relatives informed her that the women were dissecting Murphy as they did the dishes.

"— Plenty of women before, until he got himself engaged to that actress —"

"— Seemed nice enough to me —"

"— Wouldn't want to see Tara get hurt —"

"What a nice young man," remarked Aunt Carolyn aloud, smiling at Tara as she entered the kitchen.

"Quite a looker, too," Libby agreed, grinning broadly.

Tara made no reply, but opened a drawer and began rooting among the kitchen linens. "Where's a towel? I'll dry."

"We've almost finished," her mother said. "Why don't you run change out of your good clothes?"

Tara agreed gratefully, eager to avoid the inquisition that had seemed imminent. But it appeared her mother had other plans. No sooner had Tara tugged on a pair of blue jeans and pulled a UNAM sweatshirt over her head than a knock sounded on the door of her garage apartment.

"Tara, can I come in?"

"Sure, Mom," she called. "It's open."

Dianne Bentley entered the small apartment and closed the door securely behind her. "Tara, I wanted to talk to you about Murphy Masters."

"What about him?"

"He had quite a reputation in his day, you know. I just don't want to see you getting in over your head."

Tara busied herself with hanging up the dress she'd just taken off. "I don't know what you mean." Even as she said the words, Tara could feel the heat rising to her face and knew her mother was not fooled. "Mom, he's my boss. Nothing more."

"I hope so. Still, there's something very appealing about a man with a troubled past," Dianne Bentley observed. "They tend to fill girls' heads with romantic ideas about the 'love of a good woman.' You know what I mean."

Tara grinned. "Maybe you'd better warn Grandma. She seems pretty smitten with him."

"Your grandmother loves anyone who'll pay her a little attention — which Murphy did, with a vengeance. Just be careful, Tara. That's all I ask."

"Not to worry, Mom. I've never found jocks all that appealing."

At least, whispered a small voice in her brain, *not until now.*

CHAPTER 8

As his sleek red car neared the *Herald* office, Murphy eased his foot off the accelerator in a futile effort to delay the moment he would see Tara Bentley again. Kissing her had not been one of the smartest things he'd ever done; putting the moves on one's subordinates never was. He hadn't planned to kiss her, didn't know what had possessed him. Still less did he understand why he'd been dwelling on the incident now for almost twenty-four hours. It hadn't even been much of a kiss — just the merest brush of his lips against the mouth of a girl who hadn't expected it and might not have allowed it if she had. Yet something about that kiss made him want to do it again, more thoroughly this time.

His brow puckered in a frown. Now *that* was a bad idea. Business and pleasure didn't mix — especially not now, when they were finally figuring out how to work together.

He only hoped that one impulsive act hadn't jeopardized what was beginning to look like a promising partnership. He slowed the car still more, and wheeled into the parking lot. He would know soon enough.

When he reached the second floor of the *Herald* offices, Murphy discovered that Tara was already at work in her cubicle. The light from her computer monitor reflected off the lenses of her reading glasses, so he couldn't be sure she saw him at all, much less gauge any sort of reaction from him.

"Hello, Murphy," Julie called cheerfully. "How was your weekend?"

"Fine, and yours?" Murphy sought the fine line between enthusiasm and diffidence. It was none of the secretary's business how he spent his weekend. "Morning, Bentley."

She looked up at him over the top of her glasses. "Hi, Murph. Say, do you know where the high school basketball prospectus is? I can't find it."

There was no silent message in her gray eyes, no hidden meaning behind her words. In fact, she gave no indication of even remembering what had taken place the previous day.

"Uh, the basketball prospectus?" echoed Murphy, momentarily taken aback. "It's probably buried on my desk. I'll check."

"I'd appreciate it."

So she intended to behave as if it never happened. Well, two could play at that game. It was probably all for the best, Murphy assured himself as he unlocked the door to his office. The last thing he needed was a clinging vine who mistook one little kiss for a proposal of marriage.

As the office door closed behind him, Tara let out a long breath and slumped against the back of her chair. She had recognized the sound of Murphy's firm tread on the tile floor, and she'd been determined not to behave like some obsessed groupie. After all, they were both mature adults. She had kissed other men before — well, Philip, anyway — and Murphy had kissed other women — *lots* of other women, if the tabloids were to be believed. It didn't mean a thing. To demonstrate her indifference, she had kept her gaze firmly fixed on the computer monitor, not even looking at him until he spoke to her. And then, after winning this minor victory, she had babbled like an idiot over a basketball prospectus she didn't even need. Now she'd have to find something to do with the stupid thing once he dug it up for her.

To her relief, the morning progressed uneventfully. Murphy spent most of the time cloistered in his office, and on the few brief occasions when he emerged from his lair, their exchanges were courteous but distant. Then just before noon, Don's secretary came hurrying between the rows of cubicles, obviously bursting with news.

"Tara, have you got a minute? Don wants to see you in his office right away."

"Sure, Joanne, I'll be right there."

Tara lingered at her desk just long enough to save the work on her computer screen, then followed Joanne to Don's office. The door was ajar, and even before she entered the room, Tara could see a visitor seated on the black vinyl sofa facing Don's desk. He looked to be a little older than Don, perhaps in his mid-sixties, and although something about him seemed familiar, Tara couldn't place where she might have seen him before.

"Ah! Here she is," Don said, motioning for her to sit down. "Tara, you'll be pleased, I'm sure, to see an old friend."

Clearly, she was expected to know the visitor, but though the sense of familiarity grew stronger, she still drew a blank.

"It's a pleasure to see you again, Miss Bentley," the stranger said, smiling at her confusion. "I take it you managed to turn in your story on time?"

A light came on in Tara's brain. "You're

the man at the baseball game! How could I forget you? You saved my life!"

"Since you two apparently never got around to introductions, allow me," Don said. "Tara Bentley, this is Jack Bryson, publisher of the *Atlanta Messenger*. You didn't know it that day, but you were in extremely good company."

Dazed, Tara took Mr. Bryson's out-stretched hand. "No, sir, I didn't. And I'm glad, because I would have felt twice as incompetent as I already did."

"Believe me, young lady, you had no need," he assured her. "I thought you showed considerable initiative that day. In fact, I made it a point to keep up with your career."

"But how did you know who I was? I never told you my name."

Jack Bryson smiled. "Forgive me, but it wasn't difficult, in the wake of the Lamborino episode."

"Oh, that!" Tara groaned, embarrassed.

"Yes, that." Bryson chuckled. "I said at the time you were one to watch. I haven't been disappointed."

"I'm flattered you think so. But what brings you to Harper's Corners?"

"You," he said simply. "I'd like to take you to lunch, if you're willing."

Tara glanced at the clock behind Don's desk. It read twenty minutes to twelve.

"Go ahead, Tara," Don urged, correctly interpreting her silent question.

"But Murphy will expect me —"

"I'll take care of him. You just go and enjoy yourself. And take all the time you need," he added as Jack Bryson led Tara from the room.

Don scowled thoughtfully into space for a moment, then picked up the telephone and punched a single button.

"Yeah?" Murphy's voice came through the line.

"Come here a minute, Murphy, will you? Oh, and if you see Tara leaving with a man, don't sweat it. I gave her permission to leave early."

Soon approaching footsteps caused the floor to vibrate, and a moment later Murphy entered the office.

"What's up? Where's Bentley going?"

"Jack Bryson dropped by to invite her to lunch."

"What?" demanded Murphy. "He's old enough to be her grandfather!"

"I didn't say it was a social visit. Do you know who Jack Bryson is?"

"No, I can't say that I do," Murphy admitted grudgingly. He only knew Jack Bryson

119

was Tara's lunch date, and that was enough for him to dislike the man on sight.

"He's the owner and publisher of the *Atlanta Messenger*," Don explained. After a pointed pause, he added, "He's also the kindly old gentleman who sat next to Tara that day at the baseball game."

Murphy let out a low whistle. "I'll say this much for her: she does have a knack for landing on her feet."

Don toyed with an ink pen lying on his desk, all the while watching Murphy surreptitiously out of the corner of his eye. "I wouldn't be surprised if he makes her a job offer."

Murphy gave a snort of derision. "She'll turn him down flat," he predicted.

Don's eyebrows arched inquiringly. "You think so?"

"Why shouldn't she?" Murphy asked, his voice rising on a note of desperation. "She's got a good, steady job here, and a popular weekly column —"

"Why would she give up the chance to cover high school sports for a job with a major daily in a big city?" Don asked dryly. "I'd say the answer was obvious — unless you know of some other reason she would choose to stay?"

Murphy flushed a dull red, and Don realized he'd stumbled onto something interesting. Before he could press the issue, however, Murphy rushed into speech. "Can't you do something to make her stay? Give her a fat pay raise, or a promotion?"

"Hmm." Don stroked his chin thoughtfully, as if considering the matter. "I could always promote her to sports editor."

"Ha, ha, you crack me up. Seriously, Don, you're not just going to let her go, are you?"

"Not only would I let her go, I would wish her all the best."

"Well, that's a fine way for her to show gratitude, after all you've done for her!"

"All I've done for her, as you put it, was to give her a chance to get a little experience just in case this kind of opportunity came along. Jim and Dianne Bentley are good people, but I always thought they kept that girl on too short a leash. She's capable of bigger things than this town can offer. She deserves the chance to try her wings."

"You can't let her do that!" Murphy protested. "We've got a column to write. You were even thinking of having it syndicated!"

"True, but nothing has been done that can't be put on hold for a while."

That got Murphy's attention. "On hold?"

"While we train Tara's replacement," Don

went on. "There are other sports reporters, you know. Who knows? I might decide to forget the column and hire another man instead. That's what you wanted in the first place, isn't it?"

Murphy nodded, but Don detected a distinct lack of enthusiasm.

"I have a confession to make," Jack Bryson told Tara after they were comfortably ensconced in a red vinyl booth, sampling Monday's special soup-and-salad combo. "Delightful as I find your company, I didn't come all this way just to take you to lunch."

"I didn't think you had," Tara admitted. "But for the life of me, I can't imagine what would have brought you all the way to Harper's Corners. Not that it's any of my business," she added quickly.

"Oh, but it is your business. You see, I've had a job opening come up at the *Messenger.* It's nothing glamorous, I'm afraid, just an entry-level position. But who knows what opportunities it might open up for the right person, with talent and hard work?"

"And you want *me* for the job?" Tara gestured toward her chest, and almost stabbed herself with the fork she'd forgotten she was holding.

"Very much. That day at the baseball

game, you demonstrated that you were dedicated and innovative. I like that in an employee."

Tara's brain spun as Bryson outlined wages and benefits. She'd told him that day that he was an answer to prayer, but she never dreamed she was making a prophetic statement. To think that one of the worst days of her life had actually been the best! She vaguely recalled a verse of scripture about entertaining angels unawares. Well, Mr. Bryson wasn't really an angel, and she wasn't sure how entertaining she'd been, but the principle still applied. She had been face to face with her ticket out of Harper's Corners, and she hadn't even known it. She could hardly believe it, even now.

"Well, Miss Bentley," Jack Bryson concluded, "what do you say?"

"I — You've left me speechless." Tara shook her head as if to clear it. "I don't know what to say!"

He smiled at her confusion. "That's easy. Just say yes."

"All right," Tara said, grinning broadly. "Yes!"

When she returned to the *Herald* office to tell Don the good news and to give two weeks' notice, Tara found both him and

Murphy in Don's office, looking for all the world as if they were expecting her. For one split second, she wondered how much they already knew, or had guessed, about the reason for Jack Bryson's visit. Then she dismissed the thought as ridiculous. Murphy looked like a thundercloud, and if he'd even suspected she was leaving he would have been dancing in the street.

"Don, Murphy, you'll never guess!" she announced, glancing from Don's smiling, expectant face to Murphy's scowling one. "I've been offered a job at the *Atlanta Messenger*! I'll start two weeks from next Monday. If that's okay with you, Don," she added hastily.

"I think it's terrific," he assured her. "I don't know who to congratulate, you or Jack."

Murphy had no such uncertainty. "Congratulations," he said tersely, and left Don's office without another word.

Tara blinked after him in surprise. "I thought Murphy would be ecstatic," she said. "What's eating him?"

Don's only response was a noncommittal shrug. "I was hoping *you* could tell *me*."

CHAPTER 9

The next two weeks passed in a blur of preparations. At home in the evenings, Tara made lists and checked them off as she packed her belongings in cardboard boxes. She and her father had even managed to squeeze in a weekend trip to Atlanta, where she'd located a small but conveniently located apartment with reasonable rent. But it wasn't until she met the college student who would soon be moving into her garage apartment that reality began to set in. It was really happening! She had prayed for this day for most of her life, and now that her prayers had been answered, it was almost like a miracle.

With so much to do and so little time to do it in, it was easy to ignore the soft voice that whispered to her from time to time, warning her that miracles were not always what they seemed. Late at night, however, when there were no other noises to drown it out, it returned, always asking the same question: *Is this really what you want?*

"Of course it is," Tara chided herself, punching the pillows into a more comfortable shape. She had lived in Harper's Corners all her life, and even now that she was grown, she still lived within a stone's throw of her parents' house. Surely anyone about to make a major life change would have a few last-minute jitters. She didn't doubt for one minute that they would all disappear on Saturday morning when she hit Interstate 20, towing her life behind her in a rented U-Haul trailer. But even so, the little voice was never completely silenced, at least not for very long.

Morning brought new concerns. Don had begun interviewing applicants for Tara's position, occasionally bringing potential employees to meet Murphy. Tara was glad no one sought her opinion on the prospective hires; she hadn't been overly impressed with either of the two girls who had come in for interviews and spent most of their time gushing over Murphy. Tara was glad she wouldn't be around to watch them on a daily basis.

In the meantime, she and Murphy maintained a polite but impersonal partnership, doing what was necessary to produce their weekly column but spending as little time in each other's company as possible. He had not come to church again, and there had been no more mention of family dinners. She told herself it was better this way, and thanked God for removing her from Harper's Corners before their relationship — if that was the word for it — could become any more complicated.

And yet Tara was aware of a certain lack of closure, a sense of unfinished business that added to her ambiguous feelings about the approaching move. She couldn't understand it. She'd lived for this day since high school, and yet every morning, as she tore yesterday's page off her desktop calendar, she was uncomfortably aware of time passing by too quickly.

The feeling intensified day by day, until at last Friday dawned, and with it Tara's last day at the *Harper's Corners Herald.* She had worked hard over the last two weeks to make sure everything was done, so there was very little left to do on her last day but clean out her cubicle and accept the congratulations and good wishes of the rest of the staff. Don Wainwright took her out to lunch on his expense account, and as they waited for the check, he reached across the table to pat her hand.

"You know I wish you all the best, Tara," he said, "but if it doesn't work out, if you ever want to come back, I want you to know there will always be a place for you here."

Disconcerted by his too-perceptive gaze, Tara looked down at her plate and pushed the crumbs around with her fork. "Thanks, Don, but it isn't necessary. I'll be fine."

He smiled, erasing the searching look that had made her so uncomfortable. "I don't doubt it for a minute. Now, if you're finished, we'd better get back to the office. I'm sure you'll have a lot to do this afternoon."

By the time the clock struck five, Tara's cubicle was a model of spartan neatness. Everything that had once distinguished it as hers was packed away in a single cardboard box. Tara turned the computer off for the last time and stooped to retrieve the box from the floor.

"Ugh!" The box was deceptively small. She hadn't expected it to be so heavy.

"Got a problem?"

Pushing her straight auburn hair out of her eyes, Tara looked up and saw Murphy leaning against the partition. "It's amazing how much stuff you can accumulate in just a couple of months."

"Here, I'll get that."

Tara moved aside. "Be careful. It's heavier

than it looks."

She could have saved her breath. Murphy lifted the box effortlessly and set it on his shoulder. "Where to?"

"My car. I'm parked out front today."

Neither said a word as Tara led the way to where the car was parallel-parked in front of the building. She opened the trunk, and Murphy set the box inside.

"Thanks," Tara said, but made no move to get into her car. Nor did Murphy betray any eagerness to be on his way.

"Look, Bentley," he said hesitantly, "if you want to change jobs, it's your own business, but if this has anything to do with the fact that I kissed you —"

Tara gave a brittle laugh. "Oh Murphy, how Victorian! We're both mature adults, for heaven's sake. It was one little kiss, and not much of one at that. It's not like we —"

"Not much of one, huh?" Murphy had thought the same thing himself, but it stung to hear her say so. After all, he had been kissing women before she was born — or something like that. "Look here, lady, you want kissing? I could show you some kissing that would curl your hair!"

Murphy took a step toward her, as if to carry out this threat, but at that moment a car drew up beside them, and a harried-looking man called to them from the open window.

"Excuse me, please, could either of you tell me how to get to Jackson Street?"

"Uh, sure," Murphy said, riffling his fingers through his hair. "Keep on going straight until you reach the post office, then turn left and it'll be the second street to your right."

"Thank you! Have a good day." He put up the window and merged back into the traffic, leaving Murphy and Tara standing alone on the curb.

Tara watched him drive away, then transferred her attention to a flock of birds wheeling overhead — anything to avoid looking at Murphy, for fear her disappointment at the untimely interruption might show in her eyes.

"I'd better be going," she said briskly, wrenching open the car door. "I've got lots to do before pulling out in the morning."

Murphy made no move to stop her, but closed the car door once she was settled behind the wheel. "Take care," he said. "Stop by anytime you're in town."

"Sure thing. So long, Murphy."

Murphy threw up his hand in a careless wave as Tara put her car in gear and eased out into the street. It was all wrong. He knew it as soon as he saw her drive away.

Tara stood by the window of her third-floor apartment, watching the rain fall in sheets from the leaden sky to the slickened asphalt parking lot below. She'd been in Atlanta for three weeks, and it had rained almost every day for the last two of them. Wiping the condensation from the window with her hand, she could see a short stretch of Interstate 20 in the distance, a dual line of white headlights moving east and red taillights heading west.

Toward Harper's Corners, whispered a small voice on the edge of her consciousness. *You could go back. Like Don said, all you have to do is say the word.*

"No," she said aloud. Her voice sounded strangely loud in the silent apartment, but it didn't matter; there was no one else to hear. "I'm not going back! I'm just depressed because of the weather. This is my big chance, and I'm not going to give it up!"

Although, if the truth were told, it wasn't quite as big a chance as she'd hoped. It wasn't that Jack Bryson had misled her. He'd told her right up front that hers would be an entry-level position. So far down the corporate ladder, in fact, that she hadn't even gotten Thanksgiving off. For once in her life, she hadn't been relegated to a card table in the corner, but had chosen the best seat in the diner, and had ordered a turkey sandwich in honor of the season.

"So *that's* it," she told her reflection, pleased to have found such a rational explanation for the depression that had lingered on the edge of her consciousness for days. "I'm going to give this place some holiday spirit if it kills me!"

After collecting her purse and a bright yellow rain poncho from the bedroom closet, she set out for the nearest discount store. She returned an hour later dragging a slightly soggy cardboard box containing a three-foot Christmas tree. A second trip was necessary to retrieve the ornaments she'd purchased, so after depositing the tree in the tiny living room, she retraced her steps down two flights of stairs to the parking lot.

Brrriiinnng!

She had just reached the second-floor landing when she heard the telephone ring. Hitching her purchases higher under her arm, she took the remaining stairs two at a time.

Brrriiinnng!

Inside the apartment, she dumped the bags in a heap and snatched up the receiver. "Hello?"

She was too late. There was a click, and then a dial tone. Tara replaced the receiver, conscious all the while of a vague feeling of disappointment.

"It was probably a wrong number, anyway," she muttered. Really, what had she expected? She'd talked to her mother just that morning; besides, Dianne Bentley usually called her daughter at her cell phone number. Her position at the *Messenger* wasn't important enough to warrant anyone calling her at home on a Saturday, and the only other people she knew in Georgia were in the singles group from the church she'd visited last Sunday. They were nice enough people, but pleasant strangers all the same.

Pushing back the wave of loneliness that threatened to overtake her, Tara heated water for hot chocolate in the microwave, then tore into the Christmas tree box and busied herself with inserting each plastic branch into the metal trunk. Whistling "Deck the Halls" as she worked, she set the tree in the window and began to decorate it with the ornaments she'd bought. It was a pity there was no snow, but snow rarely came to the deep South before January, if then. Rain made a poor substitute, but they were both cold and wet, and they both fell from the sky. Rain would have to do.

Remember, whispered that persistent little voice, accompanied by the tapping of raindrops against the window pane, *this is what you said you wanted.*

"I'm leaning toward this one," Don Wainwright told Murphy, passing a paper across his desk.

Murphy blinked the Monday morning lethargy from his eyes and studied the neatly typed résumé. The slight pucker between his eyebrows expressed his dissatisfaction as plainly as if he'd spoken it aloud.

"You prefer the Barnhill girl?" Don asked, watching his sports editor expectantly.

"To tell you the truth, I wasn't wild about either one of them," Murphy admitted.

"Look, Murphy, I don't mind filling in for a while, but we can't go on this way indefinitely. Sooner or later I'm going to have to hire somebody."

Murphy sank deeper into the vinyl sofa. "I know, I know. Don't think I don't appreciate the way you've been covering the high school basketball games for me, because I do. I'm just not convinced we've found the right person, that's all."

Don didn't say that the right person was at that moment covering stories for the *Atlanta Messenger.* He suspected that Murphy already knew it. As much as Don had regretted the demise of the "His & Hers" column, he couldn't fault Tara for grabbing the opportunity to work for a larger paper; anyone with an ounce of ambition would have done the same. Murphy, however, had responded to her departure as if he had been personally betrayed. As Murphy systematically rejected all the best candidates for the job, Don wondered, not for the first time, exactly what had occurred between the two of them to provoke such a reaction.

"It's been almost a month, Murphy. How much longer do you expect me to wait?" Receiving no answer, he continued. "I'm too old to keep up at this pace. There's a reason why God puts old guys behind desks."

That remark won a smile from Murphy, the first one Don had seen in several days. "Old, nothing! I've got stuff in my refrigerator that's older than you."

"I'm pushing sixty — pushing hard," Don informed him. "By the time I reached the top of the bleachers Friday night, my heart was pounding like I'd just run a marathon."

"You don't get enough exercise," Murphy said. "Maybe you should see a doctor."

"You're a fine one to talk about doctors! The way you limp around here —"

"It's the knee." Murphy's blue eyes assumed a blank look, as if someone inside had flicked the shutters closed. "It's been acting up lately."

Don suspected Murphy's problems went beyond the merely physical, but he knew Murphy would be offended at the very suggestion. Rather than debate the issue, he picked up the telephone and turned it around so the keypad faced Murphy.

"All right, then. Call and make yourself an appointment."

Murphy eyed the telephone warily. "Call the doctor?"

Don nodded. "Unless you think the hairdresser would do a better job."

"I will if you will."

"You've got a deal," Don said. "You go first."

Reluctantly, Murphy lifted the receiver and punched in the number. A few minutes later, the appointment made, he hung up the phone and handed it back to Don. "Your turn."

"Maybe in another week or so, after things settle down a little bit."

"We had a deal, remember?" Murphy said ominously.

Don's smile was smugness itself. "So I lied. Sue me."

■ ■ ■ ■

Stripped to his underwear, Murphy sat on the edge of the examination table watching as the doctor clipped the familiar blue-black transparencies to the lighted viewing screen. It was incredible to think that he had lived the first twenty-seven years of his life without knowing or caring what the bones in his legs looked like. Now, he reflected, he could have picked them out of an x-ray lineup.

"I have good news and bad news," the doctor began.

Murphy grimaced at the age-old line. "What's the bad?"

The doctor pointed at the x-ray, indicating an area of white below the kneecap. "This is scar tissue from the original injury. It's what's causing the pain."

"I haven't noticed that much pain — just an occasional twinge."

"That's because you've begun limping to compensate for it. You probably developed the habit so gradually that you never even realized you were doing it. The bad news is, the pain isn't going away without treatment. In fact, it might even get worse as more scar tissue builds up."

"And the good news?"

"They're doing marvelous things with arthroscopic surgery these days."

Murphy leaped lightly down from the table and reached for his discarded pants. "Forget it, Doc! If I never get cut on again, it'll be all too soon."

"Arthroscopic surgery isn't nearly as intrusive as traditional surgery, and the recovery time is much shorter," the doctor coaxed, but to no avail. Murphy already had his pants on and now picked up his shirt. The doctor plunged ahead, doing his best to present his case before his patient walked out on him. "If you'd like to have a consultation, I'll have the front desk set one up for you. I know of a man in Atlanta who specializes in —"

"Atlanta?" Murphy, still only half dressed, froze as if he'd been hit by a tranquilizer dart. Tara Bentley was in Atlanta. He had tried to call her last Saturday to ask her what she'd done with the high school basketball prospectus, but he had gotten no answer. He'd finally found the prospectus, but not before spending the rest of the evening wondering what she was doing, and with whom. If he was going to be in town anyway, he might as well look her up. Maybe then he could figure out what it was about her that made it impossible to get her out of his mind.

"Okay, Doc," he said at last. "Set it up."

CHAPTER 10

Murphy slept late on Sunday morning, a habit he'd developed in the few weeks since he'd attended church with Tara. As long as he was asleep, he didn't have to confront the nagging conviction that he ought to go back. Now, fully awake, he lay on his back staring up at the ceiling. He thought of that other Sunday when he'd arrived late, of his frank relief at spotting Tara, the only familiar face in a sea of curious stares. He'd discovered that, like Tara's grandmother, he didn't like going to church alone.

A thought struck him, and he rolled over and looked at the clock on the nightstand. It was five minutes after ten. Tossing back the covers, Murphy sat up in bed and dug through the nightstand drawer for the telephone directory. He leafed through the pages, then picked up the telephone and punched a few buttons. A moment later, a feminine voice came through the line.

"Hello?"

"Is this Libby Clark?"

"Yes."

"Why aren't you at church?" Murphy demanded with mock severity.

"Who *is* this?"

"Murphy Masters. You met me at your birthday party."

"Oh, I remember now! You're Tara's young man."

He liked the sound of it too much to set her straight. "Now that she's moved to Atlanta, I can finally admit the truth. I was only using her to get to you."

She chuckled. "You really are shameless, you know that?"

"Go to church with me," he urged. "Why knows? Maybe I'll decide to mend my ways."

"Are you serious?"

"Absolutely. I'll pick you up in half an hour."

"Half an hour?" she echoed, her voice a mixture of amusement and exasperation. "Do you have any idea how long it takes a woman my age to make herself beautiful?"

"Sorry, I forgot," Murphy confessed, then added, "Make that fifteen minutes."

Murphy could still hear her squawking protests as he hung up the phone. Chuckling, he headed for the shower.

In spite of her objections, Libby was waiting on the front porch of her small white house when Murphy drove up. Even from a distance, he could tell that she was fully dressed up and made up, with her short hair fashionably styled. He couldn't help wondering if he would have found her waiting even if he'd come fifteen minutes earlier, as he'd threatened.

"Helen Jackson will be green with envy," she chortled delightedly as he opened the passenger door of the sleek red convertible. "Can we put the top down?"

Murphy shook his head. "In late November? Better not." She looked so crestfallen, like a child denied a promised treat, that he felt compelled to add, "Maybe on the way home, just until we're out of sight of the church."

Libby's cup was full, and when they arrived at church just in time to see Helen Jackson walking across the parking lot, it began to overflow. Murphy came around and opened the door for her, then took her arm as they mounted the front steps to the church.

Not until they were comfortably settled in a pew did he turn to her and ask in an off-hand manner, "So, have you heard anything from Tara lately?"

Libby looked at the slender gold watch on her left wrist. "That was very good," she said, nodding her approval. "It took you a full fifteen minutes to ask me what you've been wanting to know ever since you called me up this morning."

Murphy, feeling the heat rise to his face, shrugged in what he hoped was a display of indifference. "Just making conversation. I'm going to be visiting a doctor in Atlanta next week, and thought I might look her up while I was in town."

"I'm sure she'll be delighted to see you."

Murphy wasn't at all sure she was right, but when she gave him Tara's Atlanta address, he jotted it down on the back of the church bulletin all the same. Then the choir filed in, and the conversation ended. Neither Murphy nor Libby spoke another word to each other until the end of the offertory hymn.

"How is it that you know all the words to the songs?" Libby asked as they settled back into their places.

"I used to go to church with my grandmother when I was a kid," Murphy answered in an undervoice.

"Why did you stop?"

"You're not supposed to talk in church while they're passing the offering plates," Murphy chided.

"You're changing the subject," Libby accused in a whisper. "And I think God will forgive me for talking, under the circumstances."

"All right, then, I quit going when I grew up and realized that life isn't nearly as simple as preachers like to make it sound."

If Murphy had hoped his candor would shock her into letting the subject drop, he was doomed to disappointment. Instead of taking offense, she chuckled and patted his hand.

"Son, when you've buried both of your parents, one of your babies, and your spouse of forty-seven years, when you're living on a fixed income and looking old age squarely in the face, then you can tell me about growing up. Faith isn't a cop-out, Murphy. It's the one thing that keeps you sane through all the rest."

A man seated two rows ahead turned back to glare at them, sparing Murphy the necessity of making a reply. By nightfall, Murphy could not have said what the preacher preached on that morning, but Libby's whispered words lingered with him throughout the day, and well into the next.

■ ■ ■ ■

Tara had just reached the third-floor landing of her apartment building and was fumbling in her purse for her keys when she heard the phone ringing inside the adjacent apartment. She ran the last few steps to her door, jammed the key into the lock, flung the door open, and grabbed up the receiver.

"Hello?" she panted, half expecting to hear nothing but a click and the hum of the dial tone.

"Tara, is that you? You sound out of breath."

Tara recognized Philip's voice and grinned. "What do you expect? I just ran up two flights of stairs!"

"Sorry. I didn't mean to catch you at a bad time."

"It's not a bad time. I just got in from work, that's all."

"Oh, yeah. I keep forgetting about the difference in time zones. I just wanted to catch you early, in case you had any plans for the evening."

"Plans?"

"You know, plans. Dates. Stuff that you can do, now that you don't have to cover ball games almost every night."

"Oh, yeah, right!" Tara agreed hastily, raking her bangs back from her forehead with her fingers. "It's great having the nights free for a change." Really great. She hadn't missed the late movie on WTBS for almost a month.

"Do you think you could tear yourself away long enough to fly out here for a weekend next spring?"

Tara hesitated a moment before answering. "I'd love to see you again, Philip, but I don't know."

"I've been thinking a lot about what you said. You know, that someday I would meet somebody else, and I'd be glad you turned me down."

Tara was touched that he still remembered, and now that she was on her own, she was getting a taste of the loneliness that had prompted Philip's proposal. Now more than ever, the idea of having someone special to come home to every evening had its appeal. Yet honesty compelled her to admit that it wasn't Philip who lurked on the fringes of her consciousness and haunted her dreams at night.

"Philip, I'm flattered. Really, I am. But I don't think my coming out there would be a good idea."

"I'm sorry to hear that." Philip sounded

deflated, but not heartbroken. "I was hoping you could come to the wedding. After all, if you hadn't turned me down, I never would have met Amy."

"Amy," Tara echoed numbly.

"Amy Newcomb, my fiancée. You'd love her, I just know it."

As Philip enumerated Amy's sterling qualities, which were apparently many, light slowly dawned in Tara's brain. Philip was in love with someone else, and was going to marry her next spring. Her chest felt strangely tight, but whether with joy or sorrow, she wasn't quite sure. "If *you* love her, I'm sure I will. When is the wedding?"

"The second weekend in May. Be sure to mark your calendar."

"I will," promised Tara. "And thanks for calling."

After replacing the receiver, she stared at the telephone for a long moment. She was happy for Philip. Really, she was. He was a great guy, and he deserved a girl who would adore him. Well, now he had found one, and Tara was so happy she could cry. As tears trickled down her face, she swiped them away with her sleeve. First a stranger had moved into her garage apartment, and now her high school sweetheart was marrying someone else.

"Well, you sure burned your bridges behind you," she muttered aloud. There was no going back to her former life, even if she wanted to. *Be careful what you pray for,* the old saying went. *You just might get it.*

Tara's gloomy thoughts were interrupted by a knock on the door. Gasping as though she had been caught in some guilty secret, she called "Coming!" then darted to the sink to splash cold water over her face, all the while chiding herself for her vanity. It was probably only the pizza boy, delivering to the wrong apartment. Besides, this was Atlanta, not Harper's Corners. People here had better things to do with their time than report to their neighbors that Tara Bentley had been bawling her eyes out.

She patted her face dry with a towel, then hurried to answer the door. Too late, she realized she still held the damp towel, and stuffed it inside one of the cardboard boxes she had yet to unpack. Then, taking a deep breath, she grasped the doorknob and opened the door.

It was no pizza delivery boy who stood there, but a tall sandy-haired man whose broad shoulders all but filled the doorway.

Tara blinked, unable to trust the evidence of her own eyes. "Murphy?"

"Hi," he said, smiling uncertainly at her.

He'd known lots of beautiful women — a few of them in the biblical sense — but seeing Tara Bentley again made him feel fourteen years old again, standing on the front porch clutching flowers for the cute little cheerleader he'd invited to the junior varsity athletic banquet. He wished he had flowers now; they would have given him something to do with his hands.

"What — what brings you here?" Tara asked.

"I've got a doctor's appointment in the morning. Your grandmother suggested I look you up while I was in town." It wasn't quite true, but it was as far as he was prepared to go at the moment.

"Oh." Was that disappointment he saw in her eyes? "When did you see Grandma?"

"Last Sunday. I gave her a ride to church."

"Oh," she said again. "That was nice of you."

"Can I come in?"

"Sure," Tara said quickly, stepping hastily aside. "Come on in. Have a seat."

"A seat" was the right word for it, Murphy thought as he entered the bare little apartment. A worn plaid love seat was the only place to sit in the small living room. The dining room was hardly better, with only a straight chair and a TV tray on long tubular metal legs in place of a table. In the window, a brave little Christmas tree strove to lend a festive air to its bleak surroundings. Murphy sat down on the love seat. Tara didn't join him there, but perched on the edge of a large cardboard box from which one corner of a blue terry cloth towel peeked.

"So," Tara said, clasping and unclasping her hands in her lap, "how have you been?"

"Fine," Murphy answered. "How about you?"

"Oh, I'm fine." An awkward silence descended, then Tara broke it. "So you're seeing a doctor in the morning?"

"An orthopedic surgeon. My doctor says I've got some scar tissue that needs to be removed."

"Surgery?"

Murphy nodded. "Arthroscopic. No big deal. What about you? How do you like your new job?"

"Oh, it's great! Right now I'm working on a story about a local golfing personality." Another awkward pause. "How's everything going at the *Herald*?"

"Fine. Don's been helping me out until we hire someone else."

"I'll bet it's a lot more peaceful around there without me," Tara said, grinning.

Murphy smiled back at her. "More peaceful, but not nearly as much fun."

He had the satisfaction of seeing the telltale color rise to her cheeks. A moment later she leaped up from her box seat.

"Hey, would you like something to eat? I'll even let you have the table," she quipped, gesturing toward the TV tray in the dining room.

"I have a better idea," he said. "Let's go out to dinner. My treat."

Tara raked through her bangs with long, slender fingers. "Murphy, I just got home from work. I'm a mess!"

"I could come back in an hour."

"Would you mind?"

"Not a bit. I'll see you in an hour, then."

As soon as the door closed behind him, Tara darted into her bedroom and flung open the closet door. She knew exactly what she would wear. She'd bought the dress in Birmingham to celebrate a promising job interview, but her optimism had been premature. The job had gone to someone else and, since there was no place in Harper's Corners to wear it, the dress had hung unworn in her closet, the price tags still hanging from the underarm seam.

As she lifted the hanger from the rod, Tara's brow puckered in a thoughtful frown.

Was she reading too much into a simple dinner invitation? She laid the dress out on the bed. She didn't know the answer, and couldn't begin to guess. She only knew that Murphy was here, at least for tonight. It was better not to analyze why that fact should mean so much to her.

Back in his hotel room, Murphy located the telephone directory in the nightstand drawer and thumbed through the Yellow Pages restaurant listings. Finding the one he wanted, he picked up the phone and punched in the number. A moment later, a deep male voice came through the line.

"Good afternoon, this is the Rooftop. How may I help you?"

"I'd like dinner reservations for two, please," Murphy said.

"I'm sorry, sir, but we're booked up for the evening."

Murphy hadn't counted on the popularity of one of the city's most elegant restaurants. "Look, I'm only in town for one night, and this is pretty important. If you have any cancellations within the next hour, will you give me a call?"

"Of course, sir. I'll need your name and a phone number where you can be reached."

"Murphy Masters at 256-555 —"

"I beg your pardon?"

"Murphy Masters. 256-555 —"

"One moment, please." There was a click, and then the mellow sound of canned music. A minute passed, then two. "Mr. Masters, I can give you a table at eight o'clock, if that's convenient."

"I'll take it," Murphy said, too grateful for the table's sudden availability to wonder at the reason for it.

When Murphy returned to Tara's apartment an hour later, the vision that met him at the door momentarily took his breath away. Her chin-length auburn hair was slicked back from her face in a more sophisticated style than the one she wore to work, and she wore a short black sheath that made the most of her slender figure and long legs. Had he once thought her lacking in looks? He must have been insane. She went beyond mere prettiness. She had that certain something that made a man take a second look, then a third. He couldn't define it, but he knew it when he saw it, and Tara Bentley had it in spades.

"City life must agree with you," he said. "You look terrific."

She smiled. "You cleaned up pretty well, yourself."

She didn't ask why he'd packed a suit for an out-of-town doctor's appointment. Murphy was glad. He hadn't thought far enough ahead to come up with a plausible excuse.

"If you'll give me a minute to lock up, I'll be ready to go."

Tara moved about the apartment turning out lights, passing through the dining area into the tiny kitchen. Murphy, his mesmerized gaze following every move she made, watched her pass the pathetic little TV tray that served as a dining room suite, and suddenly he realized with startling clarity that he wanted to see her at the breakfast table — *his* breakfast table — every morning for the rest of his life.

"Murphy, are you all right?" Tara asked, giving him an uncomfortably close look. "You look sort of strange."

He shook off the unaccustomed feeling. "It's the knee," he lied. "It pains me now and then."

"Do you need an aspirin? I think I've got some."

"No, no, I'll be fine." Aspirin wasn't the cure for what was ailing him. "Are you ready?"

Conversation was desultory as Murphy's sleek red sports car sliced through the city. Streetlights cast moving shafts of silver across the interior of the car, and Murphy couldn't resist stealing an occasional glance at the stunning young woman seated beside him. She was nothing like the women he usually dated. Most of them had lush curves and weren't afraid to flaunt them. Tara's charms were more subtle, and infinitely more alluring.

Arriving at the hotel that housed the Rooftop on its uppermost floor, Murphy tossed his car keys to an eager valet, then escorted Tara inside. A white-jacketed *maitre d'* led them to an intimate table by the window. Nearby, half a dozen couples swayed to the music of a small jazz combo. As Murphy placed their order, Tara gazed out the window at the lights of the city below.

"Penny for your thoughts," Murphy said as the waiter withdrew.

"I was just thinking we're a long way from Harper's Corners."

"Not really. Less than two hundred miles, as the crow flies."

"Spoken like someone who's traveled all over the country," Tara retorted with a smile. "Believe me, Murphy, it's like another planet."

"So," Murphy said, gesturing toward the dance floor, "do you want to dance?"

Tara arched a dubious eyebrow. "That can't be good for your knee. I don't think your doctor would approve."

"Maybe not, but I don't have to answer to him until tomorrow."

Tara shook her head. "If it's okay with you, I'd rather just sit here and talk."

Murphy nodded, grateful for the reprieve. He'd felt obligated to ask, but he didn't quite trust himself with this girl in his arms. He wasn't at all sure he wouldn't blurt out something stupid, something like *I've been miserable every day since you went away,* or *I think I'm falling in love with you.*

And so talk they did. Tara laughed at Murphy's description of her grandmother riding home from church in his convertible with the top down, and she painted for him a vivid word picture of her adventures driving in Atlanta's rush hour traffic. They talked until the candle on the table burned low, and the couples on the dance floor gradually drifted away arm in arm.

It was almost midnight by the time they climbed the stairs to Tara's apartment. As they approached the second-floor landing, Murphy's steps dragged. Had she been any other woman, he knew what would come next: a coy invitation to come inside and, if he were so inclined, a late breakfast in the morning. But the old rules no longer applied, and he hadn't yet figured out the new ones.

When they reached her door, Tara inserted the key into the lock, then turned to look back at him. "Thank you for the dinner, Murphy. I had a great time. Good luck with your appointment tomorrow."

He relaxed slightly. This was something he could handle. "If it's all right with you, I thought I'd stop by the *Messenger* tomorrow before I leave for home and let you know what I found out."

"I'd like that. I'll show you around — you know, show you how the big boys operate."

Murphy didn't return her playful smile, but took a step nearer. "Bentley — Tara —"

Her smile faded, and she looked up at him expectantly, apparently as conscious of the suddenly charged atmosphere as he was. "Yes?"

The word, hardly more than a whisper, might have been an inquiry or an invitation — or a tantalizing combination of both. He drew her close and slowly lowered his mouth to hers. Tara did not pull away, but lifted her face to his, and Murphy tightened his arms about her in response. Her slender form seemed to mold to him as if designed for the purpose. He kissed her assertively yet tentatively, his kiss expressing all the conflicting emotions he could not yet put into words.

It was Tara who drew back first, breaking the sweet contact. "I'd better go," she said breathlessly.

Reluctantly Murphy nodded and released her, studying her face as if searching for answers. But there were none to be found there, for Tara's eyes, wide and dilated, mirrored the confusion of his own heart.

CHAPTER 11

"The incision would be here, just below the kneecap, and the scope would be inserted here —"

Murphy, once again stripped to his underwear and seated on a doctor's examining table, tried to focus his attention on the surgeon's description of the proposed surgery. It wasn't easy. He kept thinking of Tara Bentley and how right she'd felt in his arms. If she had invited him to stay, he would have accepted without hesitation. But no invitation had been forthcoming, and he knew Tara well enough not to suggest such a thing himself. His lips twitched at the thought. If he knew his Tara Bentley, she would have tossed him over the balcony rail and sent him back to Harper's Corners with a flea in his ear. No, she was definitely the marrying kind.

And far from settling anything, that discovery only raised a new series of questions.

He was surprised at how much the idea appealed to him. But in spite of the freewheeling life he had once led, he now found that he was too old-fashioned to tolerate the thought of a commuter marriage. During his brief engagement to Damaris Wade, it was understood that she would pursue her acting career on the West Coast while he spent most of the year in Green Bay. Either of them would have laughed at the suggestion that the other deserved a higher priority than to be squeezed in around filming and the off-season. But the prospect of such an arrangement with Tara was insupportable. If they were to marry, one of them would have to relocate. Would she be willing to give up her dream job to come back to Harper's Corners with him? Did he even have the right to ask such a thing of her?

"If all goes well, you could even return to professional football within a year," the doctor concluded.

His words jolted Murphy back to the present. "Go back to the NFL?"

The doctor shrugged. "I don't see why not." He removed a handful of brochures from a rack on the opposite wall. "Of course, you don't have to make a decision today. Take these home with you to read, and if you decide to have the operation, give my office a call and we'll set it up."

Murphy thumbed through the brochures, which described a surgical procedure completely different from the one he'd come to Atlanta to discuss. Apparently at some point the doctor had changed the subject, suggesting that the simple removal of scar tissue be followed up with a new procedure still in the experimental stages. While he'd been daydreaming, his old life had been handed back to him on a silver platter. He should be elated, but instead he merely felt dazed. The possibility of making an NFL comeback had always seemed so far-fetched that had never even allowed himself to consider it. Now he was surprised to discover that he no longer wanted gridiron glory. He wanted Tara Bentley instead.

After he left the doctor's office, Murphy bought a copy of the *Atlanta Messenger* from the machine he'd noticed in front of the medical building. He flipped through the sports section, scanning each page for Tara's byline, but didn't see her name anywhere. Nor, for that matter, did he see any golfing article like the one she'd described. Now that he thought about it, it was the wrong time of year for golf, anyway. He folded the paper and tossed it onto the passenger seat of his car. Later he would look at it more thoroughly. At the moment, he was more interested in the writer than the story.

Murphy left his car in a multi-level parking garage and walked half a block to the towering steel and glass building that housed the *Atlanta Messenger.* As he entered through the double doors, he blinked at the spacious, ultra-modern reception area. No wonder Tara had been so excited to get a job at a place like this. She'd have to be crazy to give up working here. He'd have to be crazy to ask it of her.

Glancing around, he noticed a young and pretty receptionist watching him with frank admiration. "May I help you?" she asked, giving him an inviting smile.

"I'm here to see Tara Bentley," he answered. "She's expecting me, but I may be a few minutes early."

The receptionist picked up the telephone and punched a series of buttons. She held the instrument up to her ear for a long moment, allowing time for Tara to answer, then returned it to its cradle.

"She seems to have stepped away from her desk. If you'll follow me, I'll take you on up. She may be back by the time we get there."

Murphy followed the receptionist to the

elevator, making polite responses to her cheerful flow of small talk. They rode up to the third floor, then walked past rows of cluttered cubicles, each containing a desk with at least one computer. At last the receptionist stopped beside a cubicle containing three computers, one against each of its three walls. Two were in use. The third had apparently been idle for some time; a screen saver image of tropical fish swam across the monitor.

"Hey, Kim, where's Tara?" the receptionist asked one of the reporters working there. "She's got a visitor."

"Ladies' room, I guess," Kim said with a shrug. Looking up from the work on her screen, her eyes widened at the sight of her co-worker's visitor. "I'm sure she'll be back soon. You can have a seat and wait for her, if you like."

She nodded toward the chair facing the unoccupied computer. Murphy noticed Tara's wire-rimmed reading glasses lying on the desk, just to the left of the keyboard. This was Tara's work station, all right.

"Thanks, I think I will," he said.

Murphy rolled the chair out from under the kneehole and sat down. He spun the chair around slightly so he could watch for Tara's return, and stretched his arm out along the edge of the desk. As he did so, his elbow bumped the computer's mouse. The colorful fish vanished, and Tara's work reappeared on the screen.

He hadn't meant to read it. After all, he wasn't her boss anymore, and what she did at work was no longer his business. But he spent at least part of every day in front of a computer, and old habits died hard. He couldn't help noticing the words on the screen: *Mr. Willard "Red" Williams, a longtime resident of Atlanta, died Thursday at a local hospital. He was 75. Williams was head greens keeper at the Whispering Pines Golf Course for over 40 years. . . ."*

The blinking curser at the end of the article drew his eye downward. His gaze followed, scanning every line as it went. With every word, Murphy's head seemed to spin faster. So this was Tara's article, the one about the golfer. No, she had never said he was a golfer, just a "golfing personality." She had given up a regular byline and a popular weekly column to write obituaries for which she didn't even get author credit. She must have hated Harper's Corners, hated working with him, more than he had ever imagined.

"Murphy! You're early. I hope you haven't been waiting long."

At the sound of Tara's voice, Murphy spun around guiltily in the chair, as if he'd been caught in the act of some heinous crime. "No, not long at all," he said hastily, standing up to block her view of the monitor screen.

"Sorry I wasn't here to meet you. I got called away. So, how did your appointment go?"

"Oh, fine," he said, attempting enthusiasm. "The doctor says I'm a prime candidate for this kind of surgery. He even says I can go back to professional football if I want to."

"And do you? Want to, I mean?"

"Hey, a chance like this usually comes only once in a lifetime. I'd be crazy to pass it up. But then, I don't have to tell you that, do I? You know all about these once-in-a-lifetime opportunities."

Tara's brow puckered in a look of puzzled concern. "Murphy, are you okay? You're sure nothing's wrong?"

"Never felt better in my life," he assured her brusquely. "I just wanted to tell you the good news before I headed back to Harper's Corners."

"You're heading back home now?" asked Tara, disappointment plainly visible in her gray eyes. "I thought we might grab some lunch — my treat this time."

Murphy shook his head. "Thanks, but I've got to get back. I've left Don holding down the fort entirely too much lately." That much, at least, was true.

"Tell Don I said hello, will you?"

"Sure thing. Don't forget to look me up when you come down for Christmas."

"I'll do that."

"So long, then."

"Goodbye, Murphy."

"Bye."

He made no move to kiss her, just gave her a casual wave and lumbered back down the row of cubicles to the elevator. Tara, watching him go, felt a wave of black depression, and chided herself silently. What had she expected? For Murphy to go down on one knee and declare his undying love for her in front of half the *Messenger* staff? No, whatever the previous night might have meant to her, it obviously had not had the same effect on him. She was female and she was near at hand, and that was it. She should have known. Her mother had tried to warn her. "Look me up when you come home for Christmas," he'd said. There had been no mention of *him* looking *her* up, at Christmas or any other time.

Tara's gloomy mood, which had lasted

throughout the morning, took a distinct turn for the worse that evening. She was just shutting down her computer for the day when the telephone beside it buzzed. She picked up the receiver and punched the illuminated button, which indicated an inside call from another extension.

"Tara Bentley."

"Tara, this is Pete Mitchell."

Tara couldn't imagine what the sports editor would want with her, unless it involved the Red Williams obit. She hoped not; she'd already turned it in, and it was scheduled to appear in tomorrow's edition.

"I hear you've been holding out on us," Pete continued.

"I don't know what you mean."

"Murphy Masters."

"How did you know about that?" asked Tara, taken aback.

"Are you kidding? It's all the buzz around the water cooler. No one ever dreamed you had connections in the NFL."

"I'd hardly call Murphy an NFL connection," Tara said. "He was my boss at the *Harper's Corners Herald.*"

"And he just happened to drive two hundred miles to see how you were doing." Pete's skepticism came through the phone line loud and clear. "I'd say that was pretty chummy employee relations."

"He was in town for a medical consultation, and decided to look me up, that's all," Tara bristled, but Pete, scenting a scoop, had apparently lost interest in her personal life.

"A medical consultation, you say?"

"He's thinking of having some surgery on his knee," she explained.

"The same one he injured? Is he planning on making a comeback?"

Tara glanced at the clock, and saw that it was already past five. She didn't want to talk about Murphy. She just wanted to go home, where she could be miserable in peace. "He might. The doctor says he could, anyway."

"And you call yourself a reporter? Get me something on it first thing tomorrow morning, and I'll give you space in Sunday's paper."

"But Murphy wasn't speaking for the record."

"He's a celebrity, isn't he? Everything he says is for the record! He should know that by now, especially if he's in the newspaper business himself." Receiving nothing but silence in response, he went on. "Look here, kid, I'm giving you the chance of a lifetime. Do you know what a scoop like that would do for your career? Or do you want to write obits for the rest of your life?"

Tara wrestled with indecision. She didn't want to betray a confidence, but neither did she want to spend the rest of her life writing obituaries. On the other hand, Murphy never said it was a secret.

"The Sunday paper, you say?" she asked at last.

"Page three, above the fold," Pete promised.

Tara took a deep breath. "All right. You'll get your story."

A misting rain began to fall as Murphy neared the state line. He was glad; the gray skies and melancholy swish-swish of the windshield wipers matched his frame of mind.

It had happened again. Just when it looked as if he might be able to find happiness, the rug had once again been jerked out from under him. He'd gotten a second chance at the NFL, now that he'd been away from it for a year and was no longer in the physical condition necessary to play the game. He'd finally found the woman with whom he wanted to spend the rest of his life, and she'd rather be writing obituaries. The people of Harper's Corners ought to erect a statue of him in front of the high school, a monument to wasted potential and missed opportunities. What was left to look forward to, to live for?

Faith, Murphy. The answer came softly, yet so clearly that the words might have been spoken aloud. *Faith is the one thing that keeps you sane through all the rest. . . .*

They were Libby Clark's words. Murphy gave a disheartened sigh at the prospect of meeting Tara's grandmother again. She was going to want to know all about his visit, and he hated to disappoint her. He knew she had hopes where he and Tara were concerned. He should know; he'd had a few hopes of his own.

Just as he'd feared, Libby fired her first question before Murphy had even closed the car door behind her.

"How was your trip? Did you see Tara?"

Murphy didn't reply until he'd climbed back into the driver's seat, closed his own door, and fastened his seat belt. "The trip was fine, and yes, I saw Tara. In fact, I took her out to dinner."

Libby beamed expectantly. "Did you? And did she seem happy to see you?"

Murphy's eyes remained fixed on the road, but his brow furrowed slightly. "She seemed happy, all right. I'm not sure how much of it had to do with me, though."

"Oh, that girl!" Libby let out a long, exasperated sigh. "That's the problem. She's *too* happy! I've spoken to her twice since she moved, and she hasn't said the first word about being homesick, or missing her family. And this from a girl who's never been away from home in her life! Do you think that's possible, Murphy?"

Murphy hated being put on the spot, especially since his observations ran so counter to his wishes. "I think so," he admitted reluctantly. "She's wanted to get out of Harper's Corners for a long time, and she loves her job."

"Does she? Well, I'm glad of that, anyway. She doesn't talk about it much to me. I guess she figured you'd understand it better than I could." She chuckled. "Maybe I'm getting senile, but I had even wondered if she was lonely and miserable, and too proud to admit it."

"If I thought that," Murphy said slowly, "I think I would be forced to club her over the head and drag her back to Harper's Corners by the hair."

It was the closest he had come to an admission of love, but it was enough for

Libby. Suddenly serious, she turned to look at him.

"I know what you mean, Murphy," she said, and he had the impression that she really did. "But when she comes home — *if* she comes home — it has to be of her own free will. Neither of us can make that decision for her, much as we might like to."

It might have been a coincidence that the preacher chose as his text Luke's account of the prodigal son, but Murphy doubted it. He suspected Libby Clark didn't believe in coincidence. He wasn't sure he did, either, but he couldn't begin to guess what God hoped to accomplish with the sermon when Tara wasn't even there to hear it.

He couldn't pinpoint the exact moment that he stopped applying the sermon to Tara's situation and began to think about his own life. He had made a profession of faith when he was thirteen, at the end of a week-long youth camp; in fact, the small church on the other end of town probably still had a record of his baptism and church membership. But within two years, he had grown from a clumsy and introverted adolescent into The Master, scourge of the gridiron. He had taken his new moniker seriously, too, and like the prodigal son, had set out in search of fame and fortune. And he had found both, for a while.

But the high school nickname had turned out to be a sick joke, for his mastery of his own life had left it a confused, jumbled-up mess. Though he had come back to Harper's Corners to heal his body, his heart and soul still wandered restlessly, unable to find peace. Now that there was nothing else left to try, maybe it was time he came home — spiritually home — at last.

God, he prayed silently, *I know it's been a while, and I'm sorry about that. I thought I could manage on my own, but — well, you know how that turned out. I'm embarrassed and ashamed to hand my life back over for you to straighten out after I've managed to make such a mess of it, but then, you're God. That's what you do. So from now on, you're The Master of my life, and I'm willing to let you make whatever you want out of the rest of it.*

Oh, and another thing: I know you're not big on giving people signs, but if you could let me know you heard this prayer, I would appreciate it.

No bolt of lightning flashed, no clap of thunder sounded. The pastor instructed the congregation to stand and join with the choir in singing the hymn of invitation. Murphy thumbed through the hymnal to the correct page, his eyes widening as the words leaped off the paper:

"I've wandered far away from God —
Now I'm coming home . . ."

"I'm impressed," he murmured aloud. And as the congregation began to sing, he quietly slipped his hymnal back into the pew rack and made his way down the aisle. Murphy's restless heart had come home at last.

CHAPTER 12

If Murphy thought having a renewed relationship with God would make his problems go away, he soon discovered his mistake. On Monday morning, the shrill jangling of the telephone jolted him out of the soundest sleep he'd had in months. Rolling over in bed, he groped on the nightstand for the receiver and raised it to his ear.

"Hello," he said groggily.

"Murphy Masters?"

"Yes."

"My name is Sam Sheffield. I'm a scout for the Pittsburgh Steelers. I hear you're planning to return to the NFL."

"Sorry, wrong number," Murphy muttered, and replaced the receiver.

The telephone rang once more as he was shaving. Although the caller's voice sounded different, it was clearly another practical joker.

"Murphy Masters? Walt Morgan of the

Washington Redskins. I'd like to talk to you about —"

"You guys are a riot," Murphy said, and hung up.

He couldn't understand it. He'd gotten a few prank calls after his injury, but celebrity, he'd discovered, was a fleeting thing. He'd been all but forgotten in the NFL; why would anyone bother him now?

The first glimmer of understanding came when he arrived at work and saw Don Wainwright waiting beside his desk, rhythmically slapping a rolled-up newspaper against the palm of his hand. Murphy was struck by how tired and run-down the older man looked, but before he could voice his concerns, Don threw the first punch.

"Well, Murphy, it looks like the boss is always the last to know."

Murphy frowned, not at all sure he liked the implication that he was somehow holding out on the man who had given him a job when he'd desperately needed a reason to get out of bed in the morning. "The last to know what? What are you talking about?"

Don unrolled the newspaper and handed it to him. The first thing he saw was his own face. It was a file photo, and it was a couple of years old, but Murphy found more to interest him in the headline, which read,

" 'The Master' Returns to NFL." It had an Atlanta dateline, and the byline read, "Tara Bentley, Staff Reporter."

Murphy stared at it for a long moment without saying a word. Faintly, as if from a long distance, he heard Don's voice.

"Is it true, Murphy? I can't imagine Tara writing such a thing without good reason."

Yes, Murphy guessed he had implied that he meant to attempt a comeback. Maybe he'd even said so outright. He couldn't remember for sure. He'd just been babbling something, anything, to let her know that he was getting along just fine without her, that he didn't miss her at all, that he didn't care if she preferred writing obituaries in Atlanta to coming back to Harper's Corners with him. And while he'd been behaving like a teenager trying to impress his latest crush, she'd been looking out for the main chance.

"Murphy?" Don asked again. "Are you planning to return to football?"

Murphy forced a laugh. "Are you kidding? I've been out for over a year. Even if I were to announce a comeback, the biggest response I'd get would be a collective yawn — along with a few prank calls, apparently."

Don scowled. "Prank calls?"

"From some clowns pretending to be

177

NFL scouts. I've had two of them already this morning." He glanced down at the newspaper. "If I'd known about this, I would have unplugged my answering machine."

Don didn't seem amused. "Murphy, what if they weren't pretending?

"They had to be. Those people probably don't even remember my name."

"You've got a couple of Pro Bowl rings that might suggest otherwise," Don pointed out. "Murphy, I don't know what happened between you and Tara, and I'm not going to ask. But if you've ever dreamed of returning to pro football — and I suspect you have — she may have done you a big favor."

Murphy didn't want to think about it. Just when he'd thought he was finally getting his life back together, she had managed to turn it upside down all over again. He didn't know what he wanted anymore. He only knew he didn't want to have to be grateful to her when she'd left him raw and bleeding inside.

He refolded the newspaper and handed it back to his boss, but it slipped from Don's fingers and fell to the floor. Thankful to be off the hot seat, Murphy bent to retrieve it.

"You're getting clumsy in your old age, Don," he quipped.

But when he straightened up, the grin was wiped from his face. Don's face was pale, his forehead beaded with perspiration. With one hand he steadied himself against Murphy's desk, and with the other he clutched at his chest.

"Don, are you all right?" Murphy asked, and immediately berated himself for asking such a stupid question. Any fool could see that Don was far from all right. "Don, what's wrong?"

Still supporting himself against the desk, Don pointed a shaking finger at the telephone. "C— Call 9-1-1."

Leaning back in her chair, Tara reached for the canned soft drink sitting on the desk beside her keyboard, staring unseeing at the words displayed on the monitor. She had every reason to be proud. In reporting Murphy's return to professional football, she had scooped every news agency in the country, and as a result she found herself whisked from the obscurity of the obituary page to a more prominent assignment in the sports department. And yet, in spite of her success, she couldn't shake the feeling that she had betrayed Murphy. He couldn't have known she intended to quote him, and he might not have been ready to make his career move public.

Why should he care? she chided herself, taking a long pull from the soft drink. After all, he was going back to his old life in the fast lane. He would be "The Master" once again, and Damaris Wade would once again be his willing slave. Why should he think twice about a female sports reporter he used to know?

She swatted at an annoying insect tickling her ear, and thunked the nose of fellow sports reporter Buzz Dixon, who was blowing ever so softly into her ear.

"Oww!" he yelped, rubbing his injured nose. "What'd you do that for?"

"I thought you were a gnat," she snapped. "If you'd leave me alone like I asked you to, it wouldn't have happened."

"Oh, come on, babe," he coaxed, massaging her shoulders. "You know I'm wild about you."

"Me and anything else in skirts. Now, if you'll take your hands off me, I'd like to finish this story before five o'clock."

"We could stay late and put in a little overtime, you and me," he murmured suggestively. "There's a big table in the conference room upstairs. Or plush carpet on the floor, if that's more your style."

"Where do I *get* these guys?" Tara muttered, rolling her eyes.

First Lance, and now Buzz. She'd been warned on her very first day at the *Messenger* that Buzz Dixon had wandering hands, but she'd never come in contact with him much, and on the few occasions she had, she'd put him in his place without much effort. Now that they worked in the same department, though, he was becoming more and more persistent, and Tara wasn't yet secure enough in her new job to raise a stink. Nor was she certain it would do any good, anyway, since Buzz already had a wall full of sportswriting awards to his credit, and knew his own worth.

For just a moment, Tara allowed herself to remember the day Murphy had defended her against Lance Lamborino, and to imagine what short work he might have made of Buzz Dixon. Unfortunately, this satisfying image was banished by the sound of Buzz's insistent voice.

"Well? How about it? You, me, the conference room?"

The phone on Tara's desk rang, and Buzz snatched up the receiver.

"Buzz Dixon, how 'bout you and me mixin'? What? Just a minute." He handed the receiver to Tara. "It's for you. Long distance. Male."

At any other time, Tara might have smiled at the idea of Buzz unintentionally using his tired old pick-up lines on another man. Now, however, she took a deep breath, trying to steady her racing heart even while she chided herself for hoping it was Murphy on the other end of the line. Their parting had been too abrupt. She couldn't accept that there might not be an opportunity to settle the unfinished business between them.

"Hello?"

"Tara, honey, it's Dad." Let alone the fact that her parents never called her at work, Tara could tell by her father's voice that something was wrong, seriously wrong.

"Dad? What's the matter? Is Grandma — ?"

"Your grandmother is fine, and so are your mother and I," he assured her hastily. "But we thought you would want to know. Don Wainwright had a heart attack yesterday."

CHAPTER 13

The rhythmic sound of her tires on the pavement seemed to urge Tara on, and she pressed down harder on the gas pedal. Her father had assured her that Don had survived the triple-bypass operation, but Tara couldn't bear the thought the he might die before she got a chance to talk to him. He had given her a job when no one else would, and she had never really thanked him for it — or explained why she had abandoned it so abruptly.

When she reached Harper's Corners just before midnight, she didn't go to her parents' house, but headed straight for the hospital in nearby Midland. The desk clerk looked up sleepily when she entered the lobby.

"It's past visiting hours," the weary woman said, stifling a yawn.

"I know," Tara told her. "But can you give me any information on Don Wainwright?

I've just driven in from Atlanta."

"Tara, is that you? So good to see you again."

Tara turned and saw Emma Wainwright emerging from the adjoining room, where the vending machines were located. The older woman smiled as if pleased to see her, but Tara noticed her forehead seemed permanently creased with worried lines.

"It's good to see you, too, Emma. I only wish it was under happier circumstances," she said, returning Emma's hug. "Tell me, how's Don?"

"He came through the operation all right, and the doctors say he's doing about as well as can be expected." She dabbed at her eyes with a crumpled tissue. "I know that if he died, he would go to be with the Lord, but I'd still like to keep him around a while."

"We all would," Tara said, giving her shoulders a squeeze.

"I was just going to grab a bite from the vending machines, but you can go on to the waiting room if you'd like. Maybe you can convince Murphy to go to bed."

Tara caught her breath. "Murphy's here?"

Emma nodded. "He was with Don when it happened. He rode in the ambulance with him, and he's been at the hospital ever since. I don't know what I would have done

184

without him yesterday — Monday, I mean," she corrected herself as she glanced at the clock on the wall, which showed a quarter past midnight. "But he needs to go home and get some sleep."

She wasn't ready for this. She couldn't bear the thought of seeing Murphy again so soon, and yet she couldn't deny Emma this simple request; she wasn't even sure she wanted to. "I — I'll see what I can do," Tara promised.

"I'll be along shortly."

As she made her way toward the ICU waiting room, Tara's footsteps echoed through the empty corridors. The only people about at this hour seemed to be the night-shift nurses, who looked up curiously as she passed. The nurses' station had been decorated with green and gold tinsel in an effort to give the place a holiday atmosphere, but the antiseptic smell could not be disguised. This was a place of sickness and, sometimes, death. The thought made Tara quicken her pace.

Reaching the door of the ICU waiting room, she paused uncertainly on the threshold. Murphy slumped on a vinyl-upholstered sofa. His clothes were rumpled and creased, and an open magazine hung precariously off his lap. His head had fallen forward and his chin, which sported a three-day growth of beard, was sunk into his chest. Something wrenched at Tara's insides at the sight of him. As she stood there debating whether to go or stay, a voice came over the intercom paging one of the emergency room doctors. The noise startled Murphy, and he sat upright with a jerk.

"Bentley?" he said, blinking at her. His first wild hope was dashed the instant he became aware of his surroundings. He was at the hospital, and it was Don Wainwright, not him, that she had come to see.

"Hi," she answered in that hushed tone which people tend to use in hospitals. "I saw Emma in the lobby. She said you were here. Murphy, you look awful. You need to go home and rest."

Murphy stretched stiffly. "I don't mind staying," he insisted. "After all, it's my fault that he's here."

The words were so unexpected that Tara forgot the awkwardness she had expected to feel. She plopped down beside him on the sofa.

"Murphy, you can't mean that!"

"It's true. I wouldn't go along with any of the new people he wanted to hire. I wanted to keep it open, just in case you decided to come back. Boy, did I get a wake-up call!"

Had he once thought the Christian life simplistic? It was the hardest thing he had ever done, carrying on a normal conversation when everything in him burned to hurt her as she had hurt him. "Anyway, Don had to pick up the slack. He's been working too hard, mostly because of me. And so he had a heart attack."

"Why didn't you tell me?" Tara asked softly.

"Why?" he asked with a bitter laugh. "Do you need another scoop for the Sunday papers? 'Murphy Masters Kills Boss!' With that kind of headlines, you'd never write another obituary."

Tara flinched as if he'd slapped her. "How — how did you know?"

"How could I *not* know? The news of my 'NFL comeback' was picked up by every wire service in the country!"

"I mean about — about the obituaries," she said, staring down at the hands clasped in her lap.

"I saw it on your computer. While I was waiting for you, I bumped the mouse by accident, and it came up on the screen." It irritated him that he sounded so apologetic. What did he have to apologize for? She was the one who had been in the wrong.

"Have you told anyone? About the obituaries, I mean."

"No. Haven't you?"

She rose and walked across the room to the window, standing with her back to him as she stared out into the darkness. "No."

"Why not?"

She was silent for such a long moment that Murphy thought she hadn't heard, or didn't intend to answer. "Everybody thought it was the chance of a lifetime," she said at last. "I didn't want them to know the truth." She expelled a long sigh. "Especially not you."

"Not me?"

She gave a short laugh. "You said all along it was the only kind of reporting I was good for."

Every trace of weariness banished, Murphy was off the sofa like a shot. He crossed the room in three strides and seized her by the shoulders. "I never said that!"

"Garden club meetings, I believe, were your exact words."

"Believe me, I changed my mind a long time ago." Ever so gently, he turned her around until they stood face to face, his hands still resting on her shoulders. "Bentley — Tara — if you're unhappy working at the *Messenger,* for heaven's sake, come back. Don needs you. *I* need you."

"Murphy, I've been gone less than a month," Tara pointed out reasonably, but her storm-tossed eyes betrayed her inner struggle. "What would people say if I came running back to Harper's Corners so soon? They'd say I couldn't make it on my own, that I couldn't hack it. And they'd be right."

"They let me in to see Don yesterday," Murphy said slowly, releasing her shoulders so that he might capture her hands in his. "His color is awful, and he's got tubes sticking out all over him. Tara, life is too short, too precious, to let pride get in the way."

Tara glowered at him. "That's a low blow, Murphy."

"Maybe, but I'm a desperate man," he confessed with a rueful smile. "If you have to have an excuse for leaving, just say you're coming home to get married."

"Why would I say anything so utterly ridiculous?" Tara demanded, snatching her hands away so he wouldn't feel them trembling. "What would I do the first time someone asked to meet my fiancé?"

"Introduce me."

Tara could only stare at him. Seeing her for once bereft of speech, Murphy was quick to press his advantage.

"Marry me," he urged huskily, pulling her into his arms. "Marry me and come back to

Harper's Corners where you belong."

Any reply she might have made was smothered by his mouth on hers, but she returned his kisses eagerly, giving him all the answer he needed.

"Am I to take that as a 'yes'?" Murphy asked at last, panting slightly as he drew back.

Tara buried her face in his broad shoulder. "No," she said, softening the blow by clinging to him all the tighter. "At least, not yet. I love you, Murphy, but it's wrong to be so happy when Don is in there fighting for his life."

"Don would be tickled pink — *will* be, next time I'm allowed to see him. Why do you think he threw us together every chance he could?"

Tara raised wide gray eyes to his. "Do you mean that Don thought — and he — so that we — Murphy, if he survives this thing, I'm going to have to kill him!"

Murphy chuckled. "No, I can't let you do that. I owe him too much. Without him, I might never have found the only woman I could ever love."

Tara's answering smile was tinged with sadness. "Except that I'm not the only one, am I? There have been others."

Murphy let out a long breath. God forgave

sins, but they still had consequences that had to be faced. He took her hands and gave them a squeeze. "I won't lie to you, Tara. There have been others, although 'love' isn't the word I would choose to describe my relationship with them. I've done a lot of things over the past few years that I'm not very proud of. But after you went away, I kept going to church, using your grandmother as my excuse."

"She told me you were," Tara said. "It meant a lot to her."

"It meant a lot to me, too. I picked back up on another relationship, one I thought I'd left behind a long time ago — my relationship with God. I've got a lot of things straightened out now. I can't change the past, but I promise I'll never give you reason to doubt my faithfulness to you."

She shook her head. "Whatever you've done in the past is between you and God. If he's forgiven you, then I have no right to hold anything against you." She paused, searching for words. How could she make him understand that she couldn't even bear to watch the commercials for *Another Time, Another Place*, couldn't see the beautiful, longsuffering Chelsea without thinking that the woman who played her had once had Murphy? "I've seen the kind of women

you're used to, Murphy. What if I can't —
what if I don't measure up?"

Murphy looked as if a weight had been
lifted. "Is that all? Tara, I don't want a
trophy wife! I want a woman who's seen me
at my worst and loves me anyway, loves me
for who I am and not what the media has
made me out to be. I want a woman who's
not afraid to challenge me, or even to fight
with me if necessary. Who pushes me to be
a better man. And if, in addition to all that,
she makes me crazy with desire for her, so
much the better."

Her blush delighted him. Most of the
women he'd known had long since forgotten how. "Do I do that, Murphy?" she
asked, suddenly shy.

He gave a shaky laugh. "You do, but that
subject is probably better left alone until
our wedding night. I only brought it up now
to rid you of the idiotic notion that you
don't measure up to Damaris Wade."

Tara's chin came up. "Oh, so now I'm an
idiot, am I? Just because I don't want to
play second fiddle to some two-bit actress
with more hair than brains —"

"Whoa, whoa!" Laughing, Murphy threw
up his hands in mock surrender. "I never
said —"

"Well, let me tell you something, Murphy

Masters! I won't cease to have a mind of my own just because I love you. I've still got plenty of notions, idiotic or not, so you needn't expect me to say yes and amen to everything you say or do."

Murphy, bloody but unbowed, caught her up in his arms. "Bentley, I'll be surprised if you *ever* say yes and amen to *anything* I say or do!"

Deflated, Tara traced the line of his bristly jaw with one experimental finger. "Surely we can find *something* to agree on."

And as his lips claimed hers, it seemed certain they would.

In the plushly appointed Riverchase Ballroom at Birmingham's Wynfrey Hotel, Murphy Masters stood at a podium facing a flock of reporters, photographers, and television cameras.

"Last month," he said, leaning slightly forward to speak into the cluster of microphones, "the *Atlanta Messenger* carried the story of my supposed return to the National Football League. That report was the result of a misunderstanding which has since been resolved. The *Messenger* reporter was young and ambitious, and based her story on an off-the-cuff remark that was never intended for public consumption. If I'd been asked at that time, I would have assured the men and women of the media that I had no plans to return to professional football."

While the tape recorders and cameras rolled, Murphy glanced down at his prepared speech. "In the days that followed that erroneous report, I was surprised and humbled by the interest shown by NFL scouts — so surprised, in fact, that I hung up on a few of them." He paused for the smattering of laughter to die down before continuing. "Because of their encouragement, I've put a lot of thought and prayer into my future. I've called this press conference to announce that the surgery to my knee was successful, and in July, I'll be reporting to training camp with the Green Bay Packers."

A blaze of camera flashes lit up the room, and the buzz of speculation rose to a loud cacophony as reporters shouted questions in an attempt to drown out their colleagues.

"What sort of contract terms —"

"Are you going to take any —"

"Is there any truth to the rumor that —"

"How do you think being out for a year will affect your ability to play the game?"

"I guess we'll soon find out, won't we?" Murphy said. Again, there was a low rumble of laughter. "Seriously, I've got a lot to catch up on — conditioning, weight training, and that sort of thing. But I've been blessed. God has given me a second chance, and I hope to do better this time, both on and off the field."

Uncomfortable whenever the subject of religious faith was raised in the public forum, the assembled media representatives were impatient to change the subject to one of greater interest, like money or scandal.

"Is there any truth to the rumor —"

"Are you going to take any kind of —"

"What sort of contract —"

"Yes?" Murphy singled out an aggressive reporter from the Associated Press. "What was that question again?"

The rest of the group fell silent while the reporter repeated his question. "Do you intend to take any sort of legal action against the sportswriter who misrepresented you?"

"Yes, I do," Murphy said, smiling secretively at a slender, auburn-haired reporter in the second row. "I'm going to marry her."

EPILOGUE

On a mild Sunday afternoon in early September, Tara sat beside Don Wainwright, twenty pounds thinner but otherwise fully recovered, at Green Bay's legendary Lambeau Field. Don's wife Emma sat on his other side. She had already brought Tara up to date on all the news from Harper's Corners, and had yielded her place to her husband so that the two newshounds could talk shop.

As Tara and Don analyzed his performance, Murphy suddenly broke through the line and sped down the field. Tara leaped to her feet along with the crowd, waving her green and gold pompom and cheering wildly, only to lapse into worried silence as Lance Lamborino dragged Murphy down just inside the thirty yard line.

"You and Emma have been married a long time, haven't you Don?" she asked, sinking back into her seat.

"Thirty-five years this December," he said with a satisfied smile at his wife.

Peering through the binoculars hanging from a strap around her neck, Tara trained them on Murphy to assure herself he was all right. "So tell me: how long will it be before my heart doesn't stop every time he takes a hit?"

"Probably never," Don said.

Tara grimaced. "I was afraid of that."

"But," he continued, "you have the consolation of knowing that he's happier than he's ever been in his life."

She smiled, knowing it was true. Murphy's brilliant NFL comeback had been the talk of the preseason. He'd been profiled in all the major sports magazines and even made the cover of *Sports Illustrated.* The recently syndicated column "His & Hers," by Murphy Masters and Tara Bentley-Masters, now appeared twice monthly in over two dozen newspapers across the country. But Tara's favorite article was the Milwaukee op–ed piece that described Murphy as a man "wholly dedicated to his sport, his God, and his bride of three months."

As "the Wave" undulated its way across the opposite side of the stadium, Lance extended a hand to Murphy and hauled him to his feet. They exchanged a few words, then Lance gave Murphy a light slap on the rear as he returned to the huddle. Tara grinned, resolving to ask her husband what the cocky linebacker had said to him — if it was repeatable.

It was funny, in a way. She had prayed to get out of Harper's Corners, and God had answered her prayers far beyond anything she might have planned for herself. As Murphy's wife, she would be following the team to some of the largest cities in the country. And when the season ended in January, they would return to Harper's Corners, the little town where she'd grown up and where, God willing, she and Murphy would someday raise a family of their own. It was truly the best of both worlds.

"Don, are you hungry?" Emma asked her husband. "We haven't had a bite since we got off the plane this morning, and it's about to catch up with me."

"Let me see if they score here, and then I'll go to the concession stand," he said, reaching for his wallet. "Tara, can I get you anything?"

Tara shook her head. "No, thanks," she said with a smile, watching with pride as Murphy assumed his position at the far end of the offensive line. "I already have everything I need."

The employees of Thorndike Press hope you have enjoyed this Large Print book. All our Thorndike and Wheeler Large Print titles are designed for easy reading, and all our books are made to last. Other Thorndike Press Large Print books are available at your library, through selected bookstores, or directly from us.

For information about titles, please call:
  (800) 223-1244

or visit our Web site at:
  http://gale.cengage.com/thorndike

To share your comments, please write:
  Publisher
  Thorndike Press
  295 Kennedy Memorial Drive
  Waterville, ME 04901